T

Research has played an important part in much of Christa Laird's novels so far. Her first, the acclaimed *Shadow of the Wall*, portrayed life in the Warsaw Ghetto under the Nazis; her second, *The Forgotten Son*, is also a historical tale, but this time set in twelfth-century Brittany. It is the story of Peter Astralabe, the abandoned son of the famous lovers Heloise and Abelard. Little is known about the boy, but this fascinating fictional account draws on period details, letters and books to piece together what his life might have been like.

Christa Laird lives with her schoolmaster husband and two children in Oxford, where she works as a Social Services training officer.

*Also by Christa Laird*

SHADOW OF THE WALL

# CHRISTA LAIRD

# the forgotten son

WALKER BOOKS
LONDON

First published 1990 by Julia MacRae Books
This edition published 1992 by Walker Books Ltd
87 Vauxhall Walk, London SE11 5HJ

Printed and bound in Great Britain by
Cox and Wyman Ltd, Reading, Berkshire

British Library Cataloguing in Publication Data
A catalogue record for this title is available from
the British Library.

ISBN 0-7445-2343-5

# contents

# ACKNOWLEDGEMENTS

It was Helen Waddell's classic novel, *Peter Abelard*, which originally gave me the idea for this story. In my research, I am most indebted to *The Letters of Abelard and Heloise* (which includes the *Historia Calamitatum*), translated and with a detailed introduction by Betty Radice (Penguin, 1974). I am grateful to Penguin Books for permission to quote from this text.

More personally, I would like to express my appreciation to Sir Richard and Lady Southern, who kindly read the manuscript and pointed out several historical inaccuracies and infelicities, and to Gill Hughes, Assistant Librarian at The Taylor Institution, University of Oxford, who so valiantly translated for me the medieval Latin of Abelard's *Carmen ad Astralabium*. Some of the lofty moral advice contained in these verses is given verbally by Abelard to Peter in this book.

Jeremy Montagu, Curator of the Bate Collection of Historical Instruments, University of Oxford, gave me helpful advice on early medieval instruments.

C.L.

*for Nigel, Julian and Adam*

# preface

Peter Abelard was born into the minor aristocracy in Brittany in 1079, while William the Conqueror was still on the throne of England. Heloise, of whose family almost nothing is known, was born in 1100 or 1101. The story of their love affair is one of the most famous in European history and has fascinated, moved and inspired scholars, poets, novelists and playwrights for over eight and a half centuries.

What *is* so remarkable about this particular love story? And why were Abelard and Heloise already legends in their own lifetime? The facts as we know them from Abelard's *Historia Calamitatum* – the account of his misfortunes, which was a sort of early version of the autobiography – and from the subsequent correspondence between Abelard and Heloise, are as follows. Abelard was a philosopher and logician of great fame and influence; he frequently upset other leading scholars with his unorthodox views, and towards the end of his life the celebrated confrontation with St Bernard even led to his ex-communication by the Pope – a sentence which was later lifted. But the brilliance of Abelard's arguments and his personal magnetism attracted students from all over Europe and helped to lay the foundations of the University of Paris.

When he was about thirty-eight and at the pinnacle of his fame, Abelard grew bored and, according to his own testimony, his thoughts turned from scholarship to more sensual matters. At this time the seventeen-year-old niece of one of the canons of Notre Dame had come to live in Paris. She was famous in her own right because of her learning and intellect which were rare, indeed almost unheard of, in a woman of that day. The girl's gift for letters greatly enhanced her charm in Abelard's eyes and he decided to seduce her. Her name was Heloise.

To achieve his aim, Abelard arranged with Fulbert, Heloise's uncle, to become her tutor in exchange for free board and lodging. But if the relationship began in a spirit of calculation and lust on Abelard's part, it quickly turned into a passionate and fully reciprocal love affair; teacher and pupil became totally engrossed in one another and it was inevitable that, sooner or later, Fulbert would discover what was going on under his own roof. After several months this happened and Abelard was forced to leave the house and carry on the affair secretly. It was not long after this that Heloise discovered she was pregnant and Abelard took her away, disguised as a nun, to his sister still living in Brittany where he had been brought up.

Later, in an attempt to make amends to Fulbert whose trust he had so shabbily betrayed, Abelard went to him and offered to marry Heloise. His only stipulation was that the marriage should remain secret. Fulbert was appeased and Abelard returned to Brittany for Heloise, who, as the *Historia Calamitatum* makes very clear, unexpectedly used every argument she could think of to dissuade him from marriage, which she was afraid would destroy both his reputation and his work. She failed to dissuade him, however, and some time after the birth of their son – exactly when it is not clear – she rode, full of foreboding, back to Paris with him, where they were married secretly in the presence of Fulbert and a few friends.

But Fulbert broke his promise of secrecy and Heloise, desperate to safeguard her husband's reputation, publicly denied the rumour that they were married. Fulbert then began to mistreat Heloise, so that for her protection Abelard took her away to the convent at Argenteuil, near Paris, where she had been brought up and educated.

At this news, Fulbert jumped to the conclusion that he had been tricked again and that Abelard had made his niece a nun in order to get rid of her. So angry were he and his friends that they bribed one of Abelard's own servants to castrate him as he lay sleeping in his lodgings. In Abelard's words: 'They cut off the parts of my body whereby I had committed the wrong of which they complained.' Shortly after this monstrous act, Heloise, still only eighteen or nineteen, agreed – in obedience to Abelard's wishes and contrary to the entreaties of many other people – to become a nun.

Abelard's *Historia Calamitatum* tells us how, after gradually resuming his life of teaching and scholarship, he clashed with the religious authorities of the day, and was publicly humiliated in an ecclesiastical trial, when he was forced to burn a treatise he had written on the nature of the Holy Trinity. This led to his withdrawal to a piece of land given him in the County of Champagne, where, with the help of a few loyal supporters, he built a little oratory and huts of reeds and thatch. He called this place the Paraclete, or Comforter, because he had found comfort there in the midst of despair.

It was not until ten years after their tragic separation that Heloise reappears in the story. In about 1129 she and her fellow nuns were for some reason evicted from their convent outside Paris, and threatened with homelessness. Abelard, by this time, had left the Paraclete to become the unhappy abbot of a lawless monastery in the far west of Brittany; he heard of their predicament and decided to offer them the Paraclete – his only property – which by now had been built into a more substantial settlement by the many students who had followed him into his isolated retreat. But although he travelled all the way from Brittany to install the sisters and establish Heloise as their abbess, we know from a subsequent letter written by Heloise herself that nothing personal or intimate passed between them at this time.

If it were not for this and one other letter written by Heloise later, after she had come into possession of the *Historia Calamitatum*, the story of Abelard and Heloise might well have been forgotten.

For what Heloise's two letters make almost unbearably plain is that the passion, for the sake of which the young girl had, without any religious vocation, dedicated the rest of her life to God, remained the central force of her existence. What is so extraordinary about Heloise is not so much that she continued to love Abelard, in silence and totally without encouragement from him for so many years, but that she invested her sacrifice to him with such enormous and sustained energy and will; for under her competent leadership the Paraclete grew from real poverty into a flourishing Order, with, as we know from other sources, no less than six daughter-houses, and a most distinguished reputation for learning and devotion to duty.

Perhaps it is scarcely surprising that a story containing such a rich blend of extremes should have survived for more than eight centuries. Yet one important element of the story *has* been forgotten. What became of the baby boy mentioned almost casually by Abelard in his *Historia Calamitatum*, simply as having been left in the care of his sister Denise in Brittany? Heloise only mentions him once; after Abelard's death, when their

12

son would have been in his mid-twenties, she writes to Peter the Venerable, Abbot of Cluny, asking him to try to obtain a prebend for the young man. Otherwise, apart from the *Carmen ad Astralabium*, some rather impersonal and moralising verses addressed to him by Abelard and written probably in the 1130s, there is a curious and resounding silence concerning him. Not once does he appear in the correspondence between his parents. It really is as if they forgot him as he grew up.

It can't have been easy, in such circumstances, to be the son of Abelard and Heloise. What follows could, perhaps, have been a small part of *his* story.

C.L.

## 1

Peter woke as a blade of light pushed in through the slit window. He heard his cousin Ralph hit his head on the sleeping-bench as he searched for his riding-shoes, and then curse as he fumbled with the shoulder-fastening of his cloak.

"Are you sure you can't make more noise?" grumbled Peter, turning away and drawing the deerskin up over his shoulders. He liked the privacy of their turret chamber, but he missed the warmth in the Hall where they used to sleep and where the fire was kept just glowing all night long.

"I'm sorry Peter – aren't you coming hunting?"

"No, Peggy's lame."

"See you later then."

Almost immediately, from behind the leather curtain, Peter heard twelve-year-old Ralph stumble on the narrow spiral stair and curse again loudly. Further down, the curse turned into a cheerful whistle. In spite of himself, Peter grinned into his rush pillow. He had hoped to fall asleep again, but there was too much noise from the courtyard below. Holding the deerskin round his shoulders with one hand, he hoisted himself up onto the deep window embrasure with the other, and watched as the hunt assembled.

The hounds were already sniffing and snarling as they milled perilously close to the horses' hooves, their breath steaming in the milky light, the chink and rasp and scrape of harness and leather and hoof mingling with the shouts and swearing of Thomas, the old groom, and the two stable-boys. This was always the best part of a hunt in Peter's view – the thrill of beginnings, the hint of danger, the comradeship – and as he watched his three cousins and their companions mount and file out of the courtyard across the bridge, he felt a twinge of regret. He saw the ease with which his older cousin Louis handled the largest and most spirited horse in Le Pallet's stable – they called him 'Esprit'. Louis was undeniably a natural sportsman but Peter hated him and resented his physical grace and strength.

The company, led by Louis, was joined by other men from the village as it turned away from the river and made its way along the side of Cow Common. Before it climbed the slope towards the woodland separating Le Pallet from the neighbouring manor of Le Bourget, Peter could just see his eldest and favourite cousin, Charles, drop back to wait for Ralph, who was already lagging behind. Peter was now aware of a delicious sense of being alone and free for a whole day. It wasn't easy to find solitude in a manor-house and solitude was something which he seemed to crave more and more. And besides – he shuddered as he saw again the scene – the last time he'd hunted he had been one of the first in at the kill. He *never* wanted to witness that again. It was one thing when a disembodied boar's head was carried aloft into the Great Hall on special feast days, tusks glinting in torchlight, but quite another to face the creature in its death throes, as slavering, scarlet-lipped dogs tore at its hide in front of its own too slowly glazing eyes.

Peter dressed quickly – like Ralph, swearing at the knot in his cross-garters. At the stables the ancient groom greeted him in his normal off-hand manner.

"Too lazy for the hunt then, Master Peter?" He was

sitting on a wooden stool just inside the doorway, polishing a pair of spurs.

"I didn't think Peggy was ready for hunting yet."

"Nonsense. She'm fine. There ain't nothing wrong with young Peggy now. You'm just lazy, Master Peter." The old man leant sideways and spat between broken yellow teeth, as if to emphasize his point.

"Yes, Thomas, I think you're right. I *am* just lazy." Peter smiled down at him, accepting the minor insult for the rough token of affection that it was.

"You go off and give her a good ride then. She needs the exercise now she'm better. But they say the river'm flooded before the ford at the Great Bend so mind you don't take her in ground that'm too heavy for her." He mumbled, apparently at the spur in his lap, and Peter had to bend down to decipher what he was saying.

"Don't worry – I'll take care of her." Peter was soon examining Peggy's near hind leg which, as Thomas had said, now bore no signs of its previous lameness. The pony pushed at Peter with her muzzle and snorted. With deft, well-practised movements he bridled her and threw his own personal saddle cloth – embroidered for him by Aunt Denise – across her withers.

"Good-bye, Thomas. Don't get too tired sitting there all day." He rode out of the courtyard, across the drawbridge, and at the crossway by the apple-orchard turned right, in the opposite direction from the one taken by the hunt, towards the water meadows and the Sanguèze. He followed the cart-track along the river, admiring the bright glances of early sunlight on the water. He listened to the thud of Peggy's hooves on the dusty track, felt the warm solidity of her belly between his knees and inhaled her rich horsy smell. Softly he began to sing and, at the end of his song, he laughed in sudden joy at the perfect September morning and pressed Peggy into a canter.

17

He followed the river for a while longer, until the track began to dwindle, swallowed up by the boggy area around Great Bend and the ford. Remembering Thomas's advice, Peter turned Peggy away from the river, across water meadows whose high grasses, woven with the pinks and purples of willow herb and mallow and cranesbill, had long since obscured the path which led up over Boundary Hill, then crossed common grazing land and eventually joined the main route to Nantes. For several miles Peter rode in this direction, the bank on his left marking the eastern boundary of Le Pallet's land. It was a high bright tumble of bloodberries (as he used to call the hawthorn fruit when he was little), bramble and sloe, tangled with foliage only just hinting at gold and the last lingering honeysuckles.

After a couple of hours he was back again at the top of Boundary Ridge overlooking the ford in the river, which worked its way through green meadows on its journey to the Loire some six miles away. In the far distance he could see some of the cottages and huts which made up the village. From the blacksmith's cottage – one of the largest, for iron was an important and valuable commodity – a wisp of woodsmoke escaped through the hole in the roof, but the manor-house itself was hidden by the continuing ridge of high land on his left. He halted Peggy, who tossed her head in protest, so as to take in the familiar view, and, as he did so, caught sight of three figures before the marshy patch around the ford. One adult in a blue cloak and two children in red ones. The bigger child was spinning round and round on the spot in an activity which Peter recognised as Agatha's new discovery – she would make herself giddy and then fall down and claim to have forced the world to turn itself upside down. I'm sure I never did anything quite so silly when

I was five, thought Peter, but then she *is* a girl.

As Peter guided Peggy down the gentle hillside towards his aunt and cousins, Denise was sitting on the almost horizontal branch of a willow watching her daughters. Agnes was picking a bunch of flowers but when she caught sight of Peter she ran towards him, the hand holding the flowers outstretched. She must have tripped on a stone or caught a foot in her cloak, for she stumbled and fell headlong into the tall grass. Denise ran after her and swiftly gathered her up to comfort her, but the child's wails were enough to alarm a family of wild geese, who took off from the water in a commotion of sunlit spray and pale brown wing.

"See how you've frightened the geese. They thought you wanted a roast goose for dinner. It was as bad as a Turkish battle-cry!"

Agnes stared after the retreating birds, already a half-smile of interest replacing her tears.

Denise, kissing the child's wet cheek, turned to her nephew. "So, Peter – not with the hunt?"

"Peggy is – well, she was – lame. I didn't think she was ready for a hunt."

"I see." Denise smiled up at him, patting Peggy's neck with her free hand. "You don't have to lie to me, Peter." Agatha ran up to them at that moment. "The sky's going to fall down," she announced, swaying from side to side.

"You are going to have a nasty fall one day, young lady," said her mother. "You saw what happened to Agnes."

"Can I have a ride, Peter, *please*?" begged Agatha, ignoring the warning. Peter looked at Denise for guidance.

"Well, wait till you've stopped being dizzy. Just stand there for a moment. That's right. Very well – up you go." She lifted the child onto Peggy in front of Peter, who enfolded her firmly in one arm, taking up the reins with the other. Agatha was a spirited, unpredictable child and Peter did not wish to take any chances.

"I want to canter, Peter, please can we canter?" she asked immediately. Peter and his aunt exchanged grimaces.

"No, you can't canter," they both said together. But Peter walked Peggy round in a circle and allowed Agatha to hold the reins in her hands, showing her how pressure on the right would make the pony turn right and vice versa. Meanwhile Denise was again calming Agnes who had decided that she wanted to ride like her sister.

Eventually, when both girls were satisfied, Peter dismounted and walked back with them along the river path.

"I thought you enjoyed hunting, Peter."

"I do. Well, some of it. Not the last part. But today I wanted to be alone."

"And instead you came across us."

"That's all right – you three."

"Just us three?" his aunt asked softly.

"Yes – no, not really. Well, you know . . ."

"Yes, I know." And Denise did know, with a sharp, sweet, sorrowful, intimate knowing, which had shadowed her since the day Peter's parents had returned to Paris, leaving him in her care – a fretful infant, less than four months old. Louis had been fifteen months at the time, a robust and energetic child even then.

Denise often wished that Peter would let her talk to him about those early days and the circumstances around his birth. He knew a few basic facts, but that was all. Sometimes she caught him looking at her almost imploringly, and then, anxious to respond to

20

his silent entreaty, she would try to raise the subject. But he always rejected the attempts; he was often openly affectionate and blossomed visibly when praised, yet there was a part of him that seemed locked right away from them all. She had tried several different approaches, some of them quite subtle, cunning almost. Now, as Agatha and Agnes ran around them in the long grass, she felt it might be a good moment to begin again.

"Peter, if you study music at one of the schools as I think you'd like to, it'll go with arithmetic and geometry, and astronomy too. I've never asked you about this before, but how do you think you'll get on with them?"

"Not very well, Aunt Denise. It's only the music that interests me."

"Not even astronomy? Of course, I don't really know about such things, but they say that these days there's a great deal to be learnt from the Arabs about the stars. I'd have thought you'd be intrigued by that – especially with a name like yours – Peter Astralabe."

Peter tensed. He realized now where the conversation was leading: this time his aunt had almost crept up on him unawares. He remembered being told when he was still very young that it was his mother who had chosen the strange, unwelcome name of Astralabe. But for what reason, he couldn't imagine. Denise could, however; she had a picture in her mind of eighteen-year-old Heloise, lying awake in her turret room – two floors above the one in which Peter and Ralph now slept – waiting to carry her only child to its full-term and perhaps wishing that the happy time of her pregnancy would last forever. With her desire for learning, she must often have longed for the instrument which would help her to fathom and understand the stars whose nightly vigil she shared. But it was a fanciful thought, and not one that Denise had been able to

21

share with Peter.

"My name doesn't signify anything – and you know I always prefer to be called Peter, anyway," said Peter sullenly. His chin protruded, his grey eyes darkened. "Besides, I don't really understand why I have to study all the subjects in the quadrivium; I just want to play different instruments, and write songs. I want to play a church organ like the one Uncle Hugh saw in Fribourg. I . . ."

"Agatha, come back from there," called Denise sharply. To Peter she said: "Peter, you need a man to help you understand all that. And, God willing, Hugh and Porcarius will soon be back from Compostela." She crossed herself as she finished speaking. Once again, her attempt to talk to him about what really mattered had failed.

"I must take the girls back now – there are so many tasks waiting for me. I'll see you later, dear. Look, your pony has strayed." Peter had allowed Peggy's rein to drop and she had wandered right away from the track, enticed by a clump of white nettle.

Peter watched Denise as, quickening her pace, she caught up with her daughters and took each one by the hand. Suddenly he was aware of clouds drawing across the sun, shutting off its warmth. The shimmering river had, as they walked and talked, become a brown and slithery thing between its lush overgrown banks. Why did nothing good ever last, reflected Peter, as roughly he pulled Peggy's head out of the nettles and remounted. Perhaps it was he himself who turned happiness sour by touching it. Perhaps it was no coincidence that he had been born in the longest and darkest night of the year – at the winter solstice. He saw his aunt stoop and gather her youngest child into her arms. He had always felt a tenderness towards Agatha and Agnes, who so openly loved him, yet now,

22

as he gazed after them, a savage envy took hold of him. *He* had never walked hand in hand with *his* mother, or even been carried by her since he was a few months old, so why should they? Denise was his aunt and she loved him, but Agatha and Agnes were *her* daughters, their blood bond closer and stronger. Surely she must love *them* more than *him*.

For he, after all, was nothing but the son of a eunuch and a whore!

He remembered precisely when he'd first heard those words, when his blood had first flamed with their poison. It had been about five years ago, when he was a boy of ten. He and Ralph and Louis had lain under their deerskin beside the fire in the Great Hall, while nearby two visitors to Le Pallet, probably merchants, had begun to reminisce about their last visit to the great trade fair at Troyes, in the County of Champagne.

"And there was gossip that Abelard the eunuch is spending a good long time at the abbey of the Paraclete, where he's installed his former whore as abbess. Perhaps they've found ways and means." Across the years Peter distinctly heard the gust of deep-throated laughter.

"Hush, Martin. You're too full of strong Breton cider. No more indecent talk of eunuchs and whores – remember where we are. Abelard's little son lies there by the fire with the others."

But it was too late. Peter had heard it all. He'd lain there motionless, staring at the shadows which played without a care on the high timber roof. At ten, he'd known the meaning of 'whore' all right. But 'eunuch' was puzzling; he'd thought it meant someone whose male parts had been cut off. So how could a eunuch beget a child? Then he thought, perhaps the cutting off had actually happened as a punishment from God for begetting a bad child.

No doubt the merchant would have been horrified to learn of the damage his careless words had done: like little toxic arrows they had lodged in Peter's heart and mind and, though often lying dormant for weeks or even months, they would suddenly – at a bawdy joke, a passage from the Bible, a minstrel's song – release a flood of fresh, stinging pain.

It happened now, as he relived those moments in minute detail: the smell of the Great Hall, made up of sweet herbs and rushes, spicy cooking, sweat, dogs and more woodsmoke than usual, for the weather had been windy; the flickering firelight; above all Louis's giggle, which he would never either forget or forgive.

Peter watched the diminishing figures of his aunt and little cousins turn left onto the track past the orchards. Perhaps it was wicked to feel so much anger, so much resentment. Had not Uncle Hugh and Aunt Denise opened their home – and their hearts – to him? Well, Aunt Denise anyway, for Uncle Hugh's feelings were less obvious. He was a good man, true to his word – everyone said so – and, as befitted a knight, he was clearly seen to follow the ten commandments. He treated the serfs and peasants of the estate with an unusual compassion, even with interest. But all the same, Peter somehow felt more relaxed when Sir Hugh was away from home.

And, after all, there were many children who grew up without their parents – some with relatives, some with no family at all – because of illness or death, or just by tradition. There was Guy from over at Le Bourget, for example, who before he was nine had been sent as page to the court of Fat Conan, Duke of Brittany, where eventually he would become a squire and then a knight. Then, at the manor of Morgat in the other direction north of the river, there were the twins, whose mother had died giving birth to them. Their

24

father had entrusted them to a household of corrupt servants and spent all his time away on pilgrimages, until killed last year in an ambush near Jerusalem. Even here at Le Pallet there was Philippe, nephew of Raymond the falconer, whose parents, it was said, had died of starvation somewhere down in the south. Louis thought Philippe was probably the falconer's own bastard son, but Peter believed the official story. Louis liked talking about bastard sons. And in any case, poor Philippe had only half his wits and couldn't speak for himself, so he was a safe subject for gossip.

But for all of *them* it was different. The point was that he, Peter, had once had two perfectly healthy parents who, even before the assault on his father, chose to give him away soon after his birth and take no further interest in him. That much he did know. Growing up at Le Pallet had been fine and it was a good family, apart from Louis. It was the silence, the lack of contact that hurt. And the worst of it was that his father, Peter Abelard, lived not much more than two days' ride away on the Breton coast, at St Gildas de Rhuys, where he was abbot.

Little Guy had been visited by *his* father. And the twins' mother couldn't help dying; that was, after all, something that could happen to any woman in child-birth. He shivered, thinking about what might have befallen their own family had Aunt Denise been of a less sturdy constitution. She was no longer young when the little girls were born and there had been a stillborn child between Ralph and Agatha. He hoped she wouldn't have more babies. Apart from the risk, he felt a sort of disgust at the thought of Uncle Hugh doing what would be necessary. He felt an unwelcome but by now familiar tightening and stirring in his groin, and he kicked Peggy into action with a temper that had nothing to do with the pony's interest in the nettles.

# 2

Over the next two weeks even Peter's dark mood evaporated in the air of excitement and anticipation which pervaded the manor. Uncle Hugh was due back from Compostela at the end of the month – God, weather and road conditions permitting – and Denise prayed twice daily in the little timber chapel for his safe return. He would undoubtedly have with him a retinue of companions from the pilgrimage, begun back in March, who must be welcomed, refreshed, sheltered and entertained before continuing on their various ways.

Charles would dearly have loved to accompany his father on the pilgrimage to Compostela in Northern Spain, but he took his position as eldest son and heir very seriously and had readily agreed that his place was at home, helping his mother to cope with the responsibilities of the estate and her young family. For six months they had shared the running of the manor with very few disagreements, but in these last days Charles had to summon all his reserves of patience not to become irked by her continual changes of mind.

First she asked him to make sure everyone was helping with the apple harvest, for the cider must be made by Michaelmas as it always had been in the time of her father, Berengar. That was a ritual Peter enjoyed every year – shinning up the trees and shaking the ripe fruit down into the willow baskets below, then staggering laden with them to the great stone press, around which

26

one of the manor's huge plough-oxen trudged its weary circle, quite unperturbed by all the noise and merriment around him.

But then Denise decided that it would be better if Charles and Louis and two of the men from the village went to the market in Nantes for more salt, which was running low as supplies had been scarce that year. Then she sent Raymond, the falconer, after them to tell them not to worry about the salt but not to forget the rice and cinnamon which, together with honey and milk of almonds, made Sir Hugh's favourite sweet dish. There was no cinnamon to be had in Nantes, and she was just wondering where to send them next when Charles pointed out gently, but firmly: "No, Mother, it's not necessary to ride for two hours to Clisson. Don't fret so. Father is bound to bring back all sorts of spices from the South."

"Perhaps you're right, Charles. You should have reminded me of that before. But what about the vines? It seems to me the vineyards nearest the mill are ready for harvesting. I know it's early but it's been so warm and sunny recently after all that rain."

"I don't think they're ready, Mother. Not quite."

"Please go and examine them, all the same. And talk to Guillaume – he's a magician with the vines. He'll know what to do." Charles wouldn't have dreamed of starting the grape harvest without consulting Guillaume, but he didn't say so.

Denise behaved in the same way with Nicolette, who had recently started to work at the manor as nursemaid for the two little girls. She was herself only sixteen, an orphan since her mother's death earlier in the year and the granddaughter of poor confused old Baudri, the retired steward, who had served Denise's father Berengar and his father before. Anxious to finish a tapestry wall-hanging for the bedchamber, Denise asked Nicolette to help her with that and to leave her other duties. Then she decided that they should after all set aside the tapestry and find the manor's best Flemish cloth, which was kept in one of the great storage kists in the Great Hall.

While searching for the cloth, they rediscovered some pewter dishes and particularly fine earthenware beakers which had been given to Berengar and his wife Lucie as a gift and which Denise remembered from her childhood. These had to be taken out and given to the servants to wash and the pewter polished, along with the rest of the best tableware. When they eventually returned to sort out the fine fabrics, which Hugh had once brought home from Flanders while on annual service for the Duke of Brittany, they had disappeared. Nicolette dissolved into tears, convinced her new mistress would suspect her of theft. Eventually, after much running up and down and wringing of hands and accusing of innocent bystanders, especially Agatha and Agnes who were the prime suspects, they discovered that Baudri had put them 'for safekeeping' in the kist which still contained Berengar's gambeson, hauberk and war helmet down in the armoury below the Hall.

"We have to keep Sir Berengar's armour clean and safe for when he comes back," he said by way of explanation to his frantic granddaughter.

"Grandfather – Sir Berengar is not coming back," said Nicolette, holding his arms and sadly shaking her head up at him as she realized that he was no longer with them in spirit.

It was not just Sir Hugh for whom Denise was anxious to prepare a welcome. Her plump brother Porcarius had also been on the pilgrimage, and for him a homecoming would be a poor affair without eel pie on the table. It had been his favourite dish since the days when he and his brothers, Abelard, Radulphus and

Dagobert (who'd been killed at the Battle of Tinchebrai nearly thirty years before) had all fished together as children.

It was therefore intended that all four boys – Charles, Louis, Ralph and Peter – should go on a fishing expedition just before the pilgrims' arrival. One morning, three days before Michaelmas, a messenger on his way to Normandy, who had agreed at a price to make the slight detour to Le Pallet, brought the news that, weather permitting, the company would be with them in forty-eight hours. He had left Sir Hugh spending a few days with his relatives near Poitiers. The fishing trip could wait no longer.

But Charles had to ride over to the manor at Les Gets, south of Le Bourget, where he hoped to negotiate the loan or purchase of another ox – one of the plough-team had become seriously lame and the autumn ploughing was in danger of being delayed. That was a problem which Charles had tried unsuccessfully to conceal from his mother, and which neither of them wanted Hugh to return to. Ralph was suffering from one of his periodic bouts of difficult breathing, brought on by the colder nights according to his mother, but more likely, according to Louis, by excitement at wondering what gifts his father and uncle would be bringing back for him.

"So you two will have to go alone," said Denise firmly to Louis and Peter, anticipating argument. To her surprise, Louis replied without hesitation:

"Certainly we'll go. But warn Berthe or whoever is doing the cooking. If we're going fishing, we'll do it properly – won't we, Peter?"

Peter's heart sank. He recognized the challenge which lay concealed in the apparently innocent appeal.

"Ye-es, I know you will," said Denise, looking from one to the other with uncertainty. "Now don't let yourselves get too cold or wet. One sick child at the moment is enough." In a very familiar gesture which Peter associated with his aunt's anxious moods, she pushed ineffectually at a lock of fair hair which regularly escaped from her wimple.

"Mother, please we are *not* children."

The best place for fishing was much further downstream from where Peter had come upon his aunt and cousins nearly two weeks before; this time they turned left at the river and walked past the manor's three strip-fields, until they reached the water-mill on Little Bend. Louis talked incessantly about things that interested him, apparently not noticing Peter's silence. He talked about the tournament his father had taken him to across the Loire in the County of Anjou the previous summer, and of his own ambition to be a tournament champion. After all, was not Guillaume de Marechal just like him, the younger son of a minor nobleman with little but his skill and his horsemanship to rely on? And did Peter know that at Le Bourget the Guiraud family had set up a marvellous new quintain? Guy and Simon were anxious to pit their skills against his in a tilting practice after the vintage, when Guy would be at home for his annual visit.

No, I didn't know, and I couldn't care less either, thought Peter as his cousin talked at him relentlessly. But at least it was preferable to his less friendly moods. Perhaps, after all, Louis was not really malicious. Perhaps he was just thoughtless, and didn't see or hear the effect of his remarks on other people. Perhaps.

Once past the mill the boys separated to take up different vantage points. Peter walked on downstream for another half-mile or so until he came to a clump of willows which reached out feathery arms almost as far as the other bank. It was a familiar spot which he liked; as a younger boy he often used to clamber on the almost horizontal branches, until once, while trying to escape too fast from Ralph in some game of chase, he had tumbled into the river shallows and, to everyone's amusement, particularly Louis's, returned to the manor soaking and bedraggled. But it hadn't spoiled the place for him. The angle of the leaning trees provided almost secret shelter where the steep bank met a little muddy, shingly beach. Peter slithered down through the long wet grasses, still lush with the greens of a late waterside summer, leaving a trail of crushed sedge and loosestrife and water-mint. He settled himself against the lowest willow branch, in a nook which seemed made for the purpose, and began to prepare his bait. Louis had complained that fishing was boring – he preferred the excitement of otter-hunting – but Peter looked forward to sitting quietly on his own for a while, without the feeling that he should be doing something or helping someone else. There was always so much bustle and activity up at the manor-house that being alone was a luxury. Yet somehow the mere fact of being alone seemed to invite unwelcome thoughts.

He wrapped his cloak tightly round him and casting his line out over the clumps of water-forget-me-not, which trailed strings of tiny blue stars in the current, he began, as always, to reflect. "Son of a eunuch . . ."

What exactly had happened to his father? Or – because he knew the answer to that, Charles had confirmed it for him – *why* had such a terrible thing happened? Was it God's vengeance? But why such a revenge? His parents had married each other after his birth, Denise had once said, so what part did his birth play in the story? At what point did they decide to hand him over to his aunt and uncle? In the last couple of years, his aunt had several times tried to talk to him about it but he had always turned her approaches brusquely away. For how could he bear to know more?

And yet he so badly wanted to understand his parents: why had *both of them* chosen to live the monastic life from which he was forever excluded? Sometimes it seemed as if everyone in the world – or certainly everyone who came to Le Pallet – knew more about them and his origins than he did. About his father anyway.

Peter was lost in thoughts such as these when he heard a strange insistent wailing sound. At first he couldn't identify the noise. Then, craning forward from his perch, he could see that just around the next bend a sheep was stuck fast in the shallows. The creature, probably immobilized as much by terror as by the suction of the mud, had thrown its head back as far as it would go and was appealing to the sky in a continuous high-pitched bleating. Peter dropped his rod, scrambled up the bank, the grasses clinging damply to his chausses, and ran back towards the spot where he had left Louis. When he was in sight he called out breathlessly, "Louis, come quickly. There's a sheep stuck in the river. I think it's one of Maud's."

"Silly old witch. She shouldn't still be keeping sheep if she can't look after them."

"How else is she supposed to pay her rent if not in fleece, then?" demanded Peter, quick in the defence of one of his favourite villagers.

But Louis wasn't interested in discussing Maud's rent. He was, however, always interested in any sort of adventure, and he needed no second demand to drop his rod and come running back along the bank towards the distressed animal. When they were level with her, Louis threw off his strapped shoes and chausses at random, and slid down the bank. Without hesitation he waded into the water, hitching his tunic up into his belt. "Come on," he shouted impatiently to Peter, who had stopped momentarily at the thought of eels. But, clenching his teeth, he waded in after his cousin, who was already groping underwater for the sheep's hind legs.

"You go to the front, and when I count to five we'll pull all four legs at once," shouted Louis. Peter nodded, but as he stooped in search of the creature's submerged hooves, he slipped and swallowed a mouthful of water.

"Try not to drown yourself," called Louis, not unkindly, but Peter was annoyed with himself. He gulped, bent his knees and then, poised for action, noticed that the sheep had suddenly become silent and still. Helplessly paralysed, it stared at Peter. Peter, who until then had thought only of Maud as the object of the exercise, felt a sudden rush of sympathy for the silly creature and, to his surprise, found himself saying:

"All right, old lady. We'll get you out of here."

"In God's name, Peter, there's no need to hold a conversation with the cursed thing. One – two – three . . ."

But it was no good. The sheep was stuck fast in the soft silt. The boys had to spread their own feet and shift their ground constantly to avoid becoming stuck themselves.

"Perhaps it'd be better if I pushed and you pulled. That way we'll be using the current. Let's try again. One – two – three . . ." There was a definite movement of the hind legs.

"Once more," commanded Louis. And this time they did succeed. They dragged the rigid animal closer into the bank before she could sink in again, and then they both had to laugh as, bewildered by her new-found freedom, she immediately resumed the bleating which had attracted Peter's attention in the first place. Then, after gingerly testing the shallows with her delicate hooves, she scrambled up the bank as fast as her uncertain legs and the groping weeds would allow. At the top she shook herself vigorously, showering Peter

33

and Louis in reward, and teetered off still in full voice.

"Well, I must say, you're a pathetic sight," remarked Louis, disdainfully picking at Peter's sodden wool tunic between his forefinger and thumb.

"You don't look much better yourself," retorted Peter, pointing to where Louis's own tunic was hanging in brown dripping folds from his belt.

Louis looked down and made a face.

"I suppose you're right." The boys grinned at each other in a rare moment of complicity. Peter reached for some weed which clung to Louis's thigh, and hurled it back into the middle of the stream. But the moment was short-lived.

"Shall we go and see Maud?" suggested Peter. "Make sure it doesn't happen again?"

"You can if you want – I've nothing to say to the old witch and I want to try and catch some crayfish anyway."

So Peter went alone to the wattle hut where the old woman eked out an existence with her poultry and her two sheep and her strips of vegetables. She lived apart from the other villagers, who went to her when they were ill and wanted advice about the medicinal qualities of herbs and plants, but who treated her with reserve and caution. She had a reputation for possessing healing powers, but had not her only child taken her own life, long ago? And wasn't it true that she had the power of seeing into the future? And was she not sometimes seen walking by the river, alone, in the light of the full moon? Denise had no time for talk such as this and trusted the old woman whom she would sometimes summon up to the house for advice, for Maud knew the plants that made Ralph's breathing more comfortable and had often helped to bring the children's fevers down. "She used to help us all when we were little," Denise had explained to Charles, who

34

once expressed his reservations about her. "And I can tell you that her goat's milk and gladiolus soothed your colic many a time when you were a baby. You've been listening to too much gossip in the village."

Peter had a particular affection for Maud. Several years earlier, he'd been brooding by the river after an argument with Louis – for some reason he'd not escaped to his usual retreat in his favourite apple tree in the corner of the orchard – when Maud had come and crouched beside him. Seeing his distress, she had distracted him with talk of how the different water-meadow plants around them could heal all sorts of disorders. Since then he had made an effort to learn the names and properties of as many of them as possible.

Maud was cleaning her wooden pails when he reached the hut and explained to her why her sheep, who had got there before him, was bleating so pathetically. She thanked him warmly:

"I couldn't manage without my two sheep, Master Peter. The cheese I make from their milk is popular in the village, and the fleece pays my spring rent for this dear old bit of land." Peter had known that she paid her rent by fleece – that was why he'd rushed to the animal's rescue – but he had nevertheless always thought of Maud as an independent spirit, who was somehow freer than the other serfs and peasants in the village, and he was surprised by the gratitude and relief in her face.

They sat down on the wooden bench against the warm south side of the hut. The river was behind them, and they looked out across one of the manor's three great fields and the huts and cottages of the village, to the gentle slopes beyond, where in the morning sunlight the beech and oak woods showed the faint flush of approaching autumn. Way to the east beyond the orchards, the manor-house could be seen nestling on its moated hillock below the ridge. Peter felt a sudden rush of love for the valley and, beyond that, the long bulk of Boundary Hill where he and his father and grandfather before him had spent their childhoods.

"But you've not picked your pears," he observed suddenly. "It's too late for the press now."

"I know. But my knees were too stiff to get up the tree this year. Even if I'd used a pole it would have taken me several journeys to carry them all over."

"Maud, I'm sorry. It never occurred to me that you'd need help. I could have done that." Peter suddenly realized what an effort the fruit harvest must be for someone so frail, and felt cross at his own thoughtlessness.

"Don't you trouble, child. Guillaume offered but I'd have none of it. I've managed all my life and I'm not going to stop managing now. I'll have a use for the pears, don't you worry."

It was said that Guillaume had loved Maud's only daughter and had got her with child. Early one morning, in her fifth month and shortly before the wedding, the young girl had been found drowned in the river. Guillaume had never married anyone else nor had he ever ceased trying to make some amends, in the little ways he knew how, to the woman who should have become his mother-in-law.

As if to prove what she had said, Maud got up and hobbled into the hut. A few moments later she reappeared with a beaker filled with a cloudy greenish-yellow cordial. "Try this." Peter did as he was bid, and thought he had never tasted anything so delicious.

"Good, isn't it?" The old woman's delight was evident in her near-toothless grin.

"It's wonderful. What's in it?"

"Ah, that's not for telling. Old Maud's special recipe. But there's my pears in there, that's for certain." She

36

scrutinized him carefully as he drank.

"And I'll tell you something else, Master Peter. It's especially good for growing children and women with child. *You've* had it before, though you might not remember, and there's many a beaker I gave to your mother herself when she was carrying you all those years ago. She would sit right there on the bench where you are now, bless her poor broken heart. Not that 'twas broken then; nay, in those days she was happy, to be with *his* child."

Peter looked up, wide-eyed with shock. For some reason he had never realized that the villagers would have known his mother.

"And you're looking at me with the very same eyes. There's no doubting it. Grey eyes they were, with long dark lashes, and they had a sad expression even then." The old woman transferred her gaze from Peter's face to the eastern view, back towards the manor-house and Boundary Hill and the Great Bend in the river. "Yes," she said, as if in touch with something far away, "too sad and too beautiful to forget."

Peter returned to his fishing in an even more reflective mood. It had never before crossed his mind that his mother might have had a sadness of her own.

## 3

It was Michaelmas night when the pilgrims finally arrived home. Charles and Louis had ridden out to meet them around midday, alerted by one of the company – Fulk, the eldest and largest of the blacksmith's four large sons – who had hurried on in advance.

Denise had put much thought into the welcome; candles glowed on prickets in all the window embrasures, family colours festooned the little drawbridge across the moat and an unmistakable aroma of roasting swan pervaded the courtyard. Peter had mixed feelings about the homecoming and the change of routine it would bring to the life of the manor; for one thing, he would have less time with his Aunt Denise and with Charles. But he could not but be infected by the general air of excitement and he smiled to himself at the thought of seeing dear, fat, jovial Uncle Porcarius again. He rode up to the top of Boundary Ridge, above the house, together with the three youngest sons of Robert the blacksmith and with Ralph, who had made so much fuss at not being allowed to accompany them that Denise had finally given in, on the condition that he wore his heavy winter cloak. Peter and Guy, the second of the blacksmith's sons, set light to a huge bonfire which had been prepared earlier and they then killed the time by running short races along the ridge on their ponies. Robert, the blacksmith, was held in awe by the other peasants, not so much for his skill in shoeing horses but more for his work as a swordsmith: Fulk and Guy, at seventeen and fifteen, were already learning the craft. Peter never failed to marvel at the size of the four boys; they had all taken after their bull-necked father and it was a wonder to him how their diminutive mother had been able to rear them. But they were a good-natured family and a lot of laughter could be heard from the top of Boundary Ridge that evening.

Suddenly Ralph, who had not joined in the races, but who sat by the bonfire eagerly watching Great Bend in the river as the evening began to darken, gave a shout.

"They're coming!"

"Race you down!" cried Guy, and the four mounted boys set off diagonally down the hill towards the river. Half-way down, with the fresh autumn breeze blowing tears into his eyes, Peter heard a plaintive: "Wait for me." Ralph was having trouble mounting his pony because of the fullness of his cloak. Peter reined Peggy in and waited.

"Come on – or they'll be home before we reach them." Peter watched the three brothers streaking down over the water meadow towards the little band of pilgrims and he knew that he was glad of the excuse to hesitate; he always felt awkward and at a loss for words on this sort of occasion. He shortened his reins to stop Peggy tossing her head.

Then he heard a short trumpet sequence, and recognized Uncle Porcarius bringing up the rear of the party with Charles. Louis was in front with his father, and in between were about eight other riders and several pack-mules.

As Peter and Ralph approached, the party reined in; while Ralph called, "Papa, Papa," Peter bowed deeply and smiled with respect.

"God's greetings, Uncle Hugh. Welcome home!"

"Thank you. It's *good* to be home, Peter. God's greetings to you, too. And Ralph, I do believe you've grown." Ralph urged his pony alongside his father, who leant over and ruffled his youngest son's unruly hair, the hood of his cloak having fallen back in the ride from the top of the ridge. After asking some more polite questions about the journey and everyone's health, Peter fell back, with some relief, to greet his other uncle.

"Peter, my dearest child, haven't they given you a single morsel to eat since we left?"

Peter laughed. "Do I seem thin then?"

"Thin! You look like a saint on the last day of Lent." But Porcarius noted with silent approval his nephew's high cheek bones and fine aristocratic face.

Peter chuckled again. So Uncle Porcarius could still be relied on to say outrageous things.

"How was your journey? Are you well, Uncle?"

"He's never been better, Peter," interrupted Charles. "He's fallen in love with Spanish cuisine – isn't that true?"

"You do me great wrong, nephew. It was the spiritual experience which was so nourishing!"

Porcarius winked at Peter and patted a rather lumpy saddle bag. "I've something special for you in here – I wasn't going to entrust it to the pack-mules, so I've ridden with it all the way from Compostela."

"For *me*?"

"Yes, for you. But you'll have to wait until we are truly home. Now you must offer your greetings to my fellow-travellers." Porcarius called to one of the other riders just ahead of him, a tall thin merchant, and a successful one to judge by his richly embroidered cloak. "Roger – meet another of my nephews."

As they turned away from the river onto the track which led past the orchards towards the entrance to the manor-house, they saw that a crowd of peasants, some carrying torches, had gathered before the draw-bridge. They had come in jovial mood, attracted partly by the promise of ale and fresh barley cakes, but also out of a sense of allegiance to a lord who was well-known in these reaches of the lower Loire for his fairness and even compassion. Perhaps some of them had come in the hope of being let off a proportion of their rents, due that Michaelmas Day. They were laughing and talking amongst themselves, some of them making bawdy jokes about the forthcoming reunion of lord and lady after so many months apart. Denise, plump now at almost forty, but still shapely and fair-complexioned, was also loved by Le Pallet's peasants for her good humour and kindness. Many of them remembered her as a spirited young 'cross-beauty', as they used to call her on account of her brown eyes and blond hair, trying to keep up with her four older brothers as they rode around the estate, and not above helping from time to time in the dairy.

And there were many, too, who were glad that it was she and her husband Hugh – whom they called 'The Stranger', for he came from as far away as Poitiers – who had inherited the estate after the eldest son, Abelard, had renounced his right to it in favour of a life of scholarship. Pious and serious like his father Berengar, Peter Abelard had been revered among the local people, yet there had always been in his bearing an aloof quality which made them feel awkward, even fearful, in his presence. It wasn't that he was unduly harsh, but his eyes had always seemed fixed on some far horizon, not on numbers of perches ploughed, or the lame hind legs of oxen, or the clearing of forest for the building of new cottages. Unlike his vivacious sister Denise or good-humoured Porcarius, Abelard had never laughed with them. And so when rumours of his great humiliation at the hands of his enemies in Paris reached the peasants of Le Pallet, the reaction had been – before anything else – one of astonishment, as if his aloofness should somehow have protected him. But by then, Abelard's baby son was already taking his first steps in the solar of the manor-house, encouraged not by his mother Heloise but by his Aunt Denise. No one in the village really understood what had happened or why; they found it strange that the lovely young woman, who had so happily passed the time of her pregnancy with Abelard's family, should have left her infant son after less than four months, and stranger still – if the rumours which later filtered back were true – that she had married Abelard in secret and then immediately gone to live in a convent. But then they had always known she was an unusual woman; a great scholar in her own right, it was said, who knew Latin and philosophy, despite her tender age and sex.

But all that was a long time ago – nearly sixteen years – and Peter Astralabe, the son of Heloise and Abelard, was now almost a man.

As they neared the crowd by the drawbridge, Peter noticed Maud standing a little apart, her small figure huddled in a cloak which seemed to swamp her. Then he saw that she was approached by Guillaume of the Grapes, a basket of what was presumably his vineyard's best fruit tucked under one arm – no doubt an offering for the returning lord – and bearing a torch in the other hand. Guillaume was obviously trying to give her some grapes but the old woman vigorously shook her head. Peter reflected sadly on the relationship between these two.

The pilgrims reined in, and Peter saw wizened old Thomas approach his Uncle Hugh, followed by the two boys who helped him in the stables.

"So you'm home, Master Hugh. That horse look as

42

if he'm needing a rest."

Thomas, who had looked after horses at Le Pallet since 1079, the very year in which Abelard had been born, was probably the oldest person in the community and certainly the only one who dared address Sir Hugh as 'Master', just as he addressed Peter or Ralph or Porcarius or anyone else. For Thomas there had only been one lord, Sir Berengar, and, though he had nothing against Hugh the Stranger, he had never really recovered from Berengar's decision to hand over the estate to the younger generation and spend his last years in a monastery.

"Thomas, there is no one, all the way between here and the Pyrenees, who understands horses the way you do." With that Sir Hugh dismounted and tossed his reins towards the old man, touching him gently on the shoulder before he walked towards the bridge.

There was a sudden quiet amid the babble, broken only by the clink of harness and the snorting and stamping of the horses. For Denise had appeared at the other end of the bridge with Nicolette and the youngest children and the women from the kitchens, all carrying torches and pressing in behind her. Seeing her husband so unexpectedly near, she dropped to one knee, bowed her head and crossed herself:

"May God be praised for your safe homecoming, my lord."

Hugh paused for a moment and Peter, watching and noticing how his aunt's shadow seemed to stretch out across the bridge towards her husband, was over-whelmed with a strange and nameless new longing. Something in his throat made him swallow; ashamed, he was glad to be able to concentrate on Peggy's bridle as she jerked her head up and down in that annoying habit of hers. The moment was brief before Hugh had crossed the short span of the bridge and raised his wife

43

to her feet; then he, in turn, knelt before her.

"Thanks be to God indeed for His great goodness. I have longed for this moment since leaving the Shrine of St James."

They embraced then, gently, politely, publicly, and walked back through the manor gate followed by the other pilgrims who began to dismount in noisy confusion, helped by Peter and his cousins and the stableboys. After them pressed the villagers, eager not to miss their share of the celebrations.

Before the celebrations began, prayers of thanksgiving for the pilgrims' safe return were offered in the chapel. Later, when justice had been done to the huge feast of freshwater crayfish, followed by green beans poached in milk, eel pies, spit-roast swan, rice with cream of almonds, apple tarts and junkets, the trestles were pushed back against the walls of the Great Hall to make way for music and dancing. Peter would have liked to concentrate on the musicians and their instruments, especially as one of them was playing the new type of cithara-harp, which had more strings than the old-fashioned lyre-harp that he had inherited from his grandfather. But he had been 'adopted' by Roger, the tall merchant in the opulent clothes who was steadily imbibing what, in Peter's judgement, was an alarming quantity of Le Pallet's own strong cider.

"I started life as the son of peasants, just like those out there in the courtyard drinking round the fire. Day after day, back-breaking work in the glare of the sun down in the south of France. Suddenly I realized that my father's downtrodden life was *not* the one I wanted for myself. God had blessed me with physical strength and intelligence" – he took another swig of cider and Peter stifled a yawn – "and so one morning I upped and left the land. I started by peddling small wares around the neighbouring villages, sometimes just flotsam and jetsam I found on the beach, and then . . ." Peter nodded politely, wondering how on earth he could escape the apparently unstoppable flow. Wistfully he watched the dancing and carolling out of the corner of his eye. Further along the bench he noticed Charles also dutifully making conversation with the rather fat elder daughter of Sir Henri of Les Gets; Louis, on the other hand, was taking part in a round dance, Sir Henri's pretty little younger daughter on his one side and Nicolette on the other.

"Then I began to meet some of the city merchants when I ventured onto the great highways, and there was one in particular who . . ."

The round swayed closer to where Peter was sitting, stirring the smoky air like a human fan. One of the women's skirts even brushed his shoe. He saw with a pang of envy how straight and elegant Louis was as he danced.

"So we eventually put our profits together to buy a half-share of a coastal boat . . ."

The tempo of the fiddle music quickened and Peter began to beat time with his foot.

". . . which helped to double our takings in no time because you can travel all through the night at sea . . ."

The tempo grew even faster, and some of the dancers began singing and clapping to the rhythm.

"But I spend most of my profits on pilgrimages to places like St Gilles and Compostela – I even went to Rome once. Travellers like us need the protection of the saints . . . is something amiss?"

For Peter was no longer pretending to listen. One of the dancers had made a mistake in the sequence and immediately there was much confusion and merriment in the group. For a second, Peter found himself looking straight into a pair of dark eyes, which laughed at him from a creamy-pale heart-shaped face. It was as if he were seeing this face for the first time and, at the sight, something deep inside him seemed to snap like a harp string. A shy smile and a toss of her long dark braids beneath their white headdress, and Nicolette's face was then obscured by Louis's tall, broad figure, as the dancers righted their sequence and the fiddle and cithara resumed their tune. With a rustle of skirts they moved further down the Hall, leaving a large patch of rushes crushed and flattened, and the merchant continuing his tale unheeded.

# 4

Much later, when the company had all eventually settled down for what was left of the night – the men in the Great Hall, the ladies from the neighbouring manors in the solar above – Sir Hugh, up in the bedchamber adjoining the solar, couldn't sleep despite his exhaustion. Quietly, so as not to wake Denise, he walked over to the window-slit and stood looking out across this beloved valley of the Sanguèze which was his estate and which he was so relieved to have returned to. All the familiar landmarks seemed to smile back at him, softened by moonlight: the well and the steep roofs of the stables on the left of the sloping courtyard, and, on its right, the tiny chapel almost obscured by the shadow of the crooked beech tree. Beyond the manor walls to the front and right were the fruit orchards, which gave way to the three great strip-fields stretching as far as Little Bend, where the river hid between its banks of willow and hazel just behind Maud's shack. Beyond the walls to the left, Hugh could make out most of the village and the dark empty patch that was part of Cow Common, before the ground rose in a black gradient which by dawn would mark, in weary autumn greens and dull golds, Le Pallet's southern-most edge. He thought of the many nights he'd spent on the road, often in discomfort, sometimes even in danger – though he wouldn't tell Denise the extent of it – since last he'd slept under this roof, and in his relief he offered up another silent prayer of thanksgiving.

There was so much to think about, to digest, from all he had seen and heard. He had new ideas he must put into practice at Le Pallet as soon as possible: new types of collar harnesses for the oxen, a different crop rotation, and he would dearly love to introduce a fruit press like the one he had seen for olives near Bordeaux. Much to discuss with Charles, and he must appoint a new steward as a matter of urgency; Baudri had clearly deteriorated very fast since the spring and would probably not even realize that he'd been replaced. He looked up at the stars and tried to remember some of their Arabic names, which he had learnt from a scholar he'd met at Roncevaux high in the Pyrenees. Roncevaux! They had lodged there on the very anniversary of Roland's death in 778. His spine prickled at the memory of the place, still alive with the legend of Roland's courage and Oliver's loyalty. Heroes from the distant days of Charlemagne. So much, so much and, on top of it all, the most recent news of Abelard. He must break that to Denise in the morning . . .

For a moment he stood looking down on her as she slept, the bracelet he had brought her, decorated with the shell insignia of St James of Compostela, still fastened to her right wrist. Like a child she had not wanted to be parted from her new toy.

As if alerted by his gaze, she suddenly stirred and sat up, all in one movement.

"My lord . . ?"

"I'm sorry, my love. I didn't wish to wake you. My heart and mind are too full for sleep."

He sat down beside her on the huge box bed. Taking one of her hands in his, with the other he tenderly smoothed a tousled strand of hair away from her face. It was a good marriage, this one that had been arranged by Denise's father, old Sir Berengar, before he retreated into his monastery. Unlike his friend and neighbour, Sir Henri of Les Gets, Hugh had not sought the company of wenches who frequented the taverns along the road to Compostela.

"Is there something wrong, that you can't sleep when you must be so tired?"

There was a pause.

"In truth, there is something in my mind. I wanted to keep it from you a little longer yet, not to spoil your happiness at our return. But perhaps I was wrong."

"Indeed I was happy. I am still. But Hugh, don't spare me now. What troubles you?" She scanned his face with sudden anxiety.

There was a further pause.

"In Poitiers I heard news of your brother, Abelard. It's not good."

"Abelard? What has happened? What *else* could have befallen him, when he has already suffered so much?"

"There has been yet another attempt on his life."

"Is he . . ?" Denise pushed back the fur bedcover and made as if to rise. Hugh restrained her.

"This was several weeks ago now and he is safe, rest assured of that. There is nothing you can do at the moment. It was, I understand, an ambush; he's slow to defend himself now because of the injury after the fall from his horse, which we knew about. But his servant was with him and defended him to the last . . ."

"To the *last*! Oh, not Thibault? Tell me it wasn't dear Thibault . . ." He nodded sadly and she buried her face in her hands.

"I can't believe this. Thibault wasn't just his servant – he was his loyal friend and companion through all his troubles. Hugh, without Thibault Abelard would have died long ago, out there in the wilds by that Ardusson river after he was . . . after that unspeakable thing happened to him. It was Thibault who helped

49

him clear the land . . . with his own hands helped him and the students to build the oratory of the Paraclete." Never slow to show her feelings, she wept openly now at her unhappy brother's new loss, and crossed herself several times.

"God rest his poor, poor faithful soul."

Hugh took her in his arms and rocked her gently, like a sick child. Abelard was not a man who other men could easily feel close to and, if Hugh were honest with himself, he had had difficulty in even liking him on the few occasions when they'd met many years ago. At times he secretly found his wife's devotion to her eldest brother puzzling, even vexing. Yet now he, too, had an inkling of the other man's isolation up there on the remote rocky promontory above the western sea. He was the abbot of St Gildas de Rhuys, where he had gone after his years at the Paraclete, and he was surrounded by hostile and devious monks, who resented his efforts to bring discipline and order to their house and who, it seemed, would stop at nothing to continue their lawless activities. This attempt on Abelard's life was but the last in a series; they had once even tried to poison him while he was staying with one of his brothers, Radulphus (known in the family as Raoul), a canon in Nantes. This time, though, Hugh had spared Denise the detail; he'd heard that a dagger had been held at Abelard's throat. The monks were rumoured to keep mistresses and to produce children, whom they supported with stolen wealth in total disregard of their vows of both chastity and poverty. The thing was a public scandal, and for Abelard it also compounded his private tragedy.

"We must *do* something. Can you go to him, with Charles perhaps?"

"Denise, I want to help him as much as you do, but remember this did happen a few weeks ago. And *you*

50

know Abelard better than I – do you really think he'd like to be seen as a victim in need of rescue? Wouldn't he consider it a further humiliation?"

Denise was quiet, fingering the intricate shell decoration in her new silver bracelet. She shook her head, understanding full well her husband's meaning. Abelard was nothing if not proud; she had once admitted to herself, secretly, that it was both his shame and his glory.

"You're right. We can't risk humiliating him any more. But Porcarius – perhaps Porcarius could go? It wouldn't be the first time he'd been to see him – for reasons of scholarship."

Of his three brothers, it was Porcarius who had been most overshadowed by Abelard's brilliance and fame, for he, too, was something of a scholar in his own right. Yet no word of envy or resentment had ever been heard to pass the younger man's lips, and he had always treated Abelard with the respect due to his extraordinary mind. Respect tempered with a gentle humour, for it was in Porcarius's nature to laugh at the world, and in this way he was superior to his brother, for one thing Abelard had never been able to do was laugh at himself.

"Perhaps we'll talk to him about it when he has rested for a day or two. He's not as well as he should be, Denise."

"He eats and drinks too much, that's why," was her immediate sisterly diagnosis. The feelings she had for her other brothers were of a different sort. "But what shall we tell Peter?"

Denise could not see, in the darkened chamber, that her husband's face had clouded. For several years now Hugh had found it difficult to exchange anything more than a pleasantry with Peter, and their reunion earlier that evening – though polite and friendly – had not led him to believe that things were going to be easier between them.

"I never know what Peter is thinking. He's always so . . . shut into himself, so remote. You never feel that with our own three boys – so different from each other, I know, yet all so easy to understand."

Denise smiled, forgetting her distress in a moment of maternal pride. "Yes, they're good boys. Charles has grown into a young man you can really trust and respect. He's lived up to all you've taught him – I don't know how I'd have managed without him while you were away."

"And Louis?"

"Louis has been – well, just Louis. Always full of life and energy and ready for a challenge. But he still doesn't make things easy for Peter."

"Perhaps the same is true the other way round." Hugh was quick in Louis's defence. He would never allow himself to show open favouritism, yet he couldn't help but admire the virile good looks, the love of danger, the easy aptitude for things physical which had been nature's gifts to his second son. Louis had been born with qualities which his father had always had to strive for, and it was therefore easy for Hugh to overlook the lack of those which he himself possessed in abundance.

"Please don't let's disagree. It was just this that caused dissent between us before you left for Compostela. My heart is so heavy for poor Abelard. Hold me close, my lord."

Hugh gladly obeyed the tender command and their whispers subsided into silence.

Unknown to them, Peter, at the other end of the house, had climbed the spiral stair out onto the parapet of the South Tower and was gazing across the valley, just as his uncle had done. But tonight, unaware of the dangers to his father's life, his thoughts were not with the strangers who were his parents, but with a pale heart-shaped face and a pair of laughing dark eyes.

Two days later, news arrived which made a visit to St Gildas, by Porcarius or anyone else, unnecessary.

Most of the guests had departed in their various directions, much to the relief of Peter – who waved politely as Roger, the talkative merchant, set off on his palfrey in his rich clothes, heading for Nantes and his coastal boat – and of Thomas, who thoroughly disliked having so many extra horses in 'his' stables and had been even worse-tempered than usual. Le Pallet was getting back to normal. Hugh and Charles and Louis had ridden out together to inspect the estate, and Peter and his Uncle Porcarius, taking advantage of the still sunny autumn weather, sat in the courtyard under the ancient copper beech, which, after pushing its way through the cobbles, leant as if tired against the manor wall. They were both absorbed in studying the gift which Hugh and Porcarius had chosen for Peter in Compostela, or rather, which Porcarius had chosen and Hugh had paid for, as Porcarius had few means at his disposal. It was a small four-stringed Mozarabic rebec, made of ebony and exquisitely inlaid with mother-of-pearl. To Peter's delight it made a melancholy, haunting sound which filled him with desire for the faraway place where it had been made – Castille – from where some merchant or musician must have taken it to Compostela. He couldn't help thinking that if there were Moorish craftsmen who could make such a beautiful object, then they couldn't be as barbaric and cruel as their reputation painted them.

"You couldn't have brought me anything better. I love it. I just hope I can learn to play it properly," Peter had said when he saw it, wistful at his own lack of musical competence. With a little help from the occasional minstrel and some from his other uncle, Raoul, when he visited from Nantes, Peter was trying to teach himself how to play his grandfather's lyre-harp.

Suddenly a clatter of hooves on the cobbles made them look up. The gate was often left unattended and the unknown man, now dismounting from a bay palfrey, had to announce himself. He was on church business, bound for Fontrevault, and brought a message from Raoul.

"Greetings, sir," said Porcarius, reaching for the scroll. "Will you rest yourself and your horse and take some refreshment?"

"Thank you kindly, but I must be on my way. I'm expected by tomorrow at the latest." Porcarius looked disappointed; he enjoyed any excuse for refreshment, at any time of day.

"A pity. Le Pallet's cider is well-renowned. But thank you for making the detour, nonetheless." Peter got up and held the messenger's horse as a matter of courtesy. They walked with him back to the gate and waited till he had crossed the bridge and turned right at the crossway, along the orchard path.

"Let's see what Raoul has to say. It might not have fatally damaged his health to ride over himself to welcome us home. But he's not one for idle chatter, is our brother Raoul – on the quiet side, like you, Peter." They sat down again, Peter immediately becoming more interested in the way his new instrument had been strung than in the letter. Without looking up he enquired absently:

"Will he visit us soon?"

"He sends greetings to the whole family – trusts we are safely arrived home – he heard news of our party from some other pilgrims we met in Aquitaine. He . . ."

Alerted by the sudden silence, Peter looked up. Porcarius was reading with a new attention. After a few moments, Peter prompted:

"Uncle?"

There was a further pause, before Porcarius turned to look at his nephew. For once words did not come to him easily:

"Yes, Raoul is coming to see us soon. And he's bringing someone with him."

Peter knew instantly and without any doubt what was coming next.

"He's bringing Abelard, your father."

## 5

Porcarius's blue eyes, small though they were in his square fleshy face, missed very little of what went on around him. He read now, with painful clarity, the sequence of expressions on his nephew's face: first, a return to his eyes of the shining eagerness with which he'd responded to the gift of the rebec; then, almost immediately, anxiety, panic even, betrayed in the gathered brow, the bitten lower lip; finally, the darkened eyes and normally generous mouth tightening into a thin line, declared defiance. And Porcarius, who knew the boy's story, who had watched in silence over the years and had understood as well as his sister Denise – perhaps even better, for he'd given less of himself – now had little problem translating what he read.

At last, I'll meet my father. We'll be able to talk together as father and son, as I'd always hoped it could be . . .

But what if it isn't? What if I can't talk to him – if he doesn't like me? I'm bound to disappoint him, not be good enough for him . . .

But why should he make me feel like this? What if I *do* disappoint him? How could he leave it so long to come and see me – he doesn't care for me, so why should I care for him?

"This isn't easy news for you, nephew."

Peter shook his head. He looked down at the little instrument in his lap, but saw it now as though through a veil, all delight in it evaporated.

Nothing good ever lasts, he thought, as he had often thought before.

Porcarius, who usually coped with the world's challenges by holding them at arm's length and laughing at them, wasn't sure what to say next. This was not a laughing moment. He would have liked to embrace the boy, but such things didn't come easily to him and in any case the moment for that had passed.

Looking up at his uncle, his eyes open as wide as possible to conceal the film of tears which had spread itself from lid to lid – for, after all, at fifteen he was almost a man – Peter asked:

"Why is he coming?"

"Because he's had permission to resign the abbacy at St Gildas. He's going back to Paris to resume his teaching."

So he's not coming because of me at all. Just a convenient overnight stop, thought Peter. But he said simply: "I see."

"I wonder if you do." Porcarius looked thoughtful. At that moment Thomas and the stable-boys appeared and settled themselves down on the cobblestones in the sunshine to clean a pile of tack, watched at a safe distance by little Philippe, who loved the horses and everything to do with them. He had been beaten by his uncle the falconer on more than one occasion when he'd been found curled asleep in a corner of one of the stalls, but the 'little idiot', as he was known in the village, was often beaten, and for lesser sins than that. Nowadays, Raymond didn't seem to care where the child slept anyway. Glad of the distraction, Peter listened to the two red-headed boys – whose father had been the village ploughman until the recent dreadful accident to his foot – teasing Philippe, daring him to come closer and 'show them all he'd got'. They never tired of making him the butt of crude jokes but their tone was not unkind and Philippe always responded with an eager, if hesitant, grin.

"Peter, shall we walk down to the river? I think it really is time to talk more about Abelard – and the past."

It was the last thing Peter wanted, but all of a sudden he knew that he could delay it no longer. One week, Raoul's message had said, and there was in Porcarius's tone an unusual note of firmness. So, after depositing the rebec and bow in the chapel for safety, he obediently followed his uncle out through the gate.

And so it was that Porcarius, who had never loved or lain with a woman, was the one to tell Peter the story of his parents' great love for one another, and of the union which had become famous throughout the western world because of its tragically abrupt and savage ending. But in Porcarius's rendering, faithful enough to fact, it was a story bled pale of both its passion and its pain.

"As you know, your father was – is – a scholar and teacher of international repute, and it was while he was at the height of his fame, drawing large crowds to his school in Paris, that he began to tutor Heloise. She was the seventeen-year-old niece of Fulbert, one of the canons there." Porcarius did not go into detail about the way in which this arrangement had been set up; *he* knew that his brother had deliberately set out to seduce Heloise, but there was surely no need for Peter to be aware of that cold-blooded beginning to the tragic tale. In such ways does the filter of truth become blocked, he reflected privately.

"Heloise lived with Fulbert after spending her childhood in a Benedictine convent at Argenteuil outside Paris. I'm afraid I can tell you nothing about anyone else in her family, but at seventeen she was already a celebrated figure because of her really exceptional

58

learning. What other woman of our time can read Latin and Hebrew and knows the literature of the ancient world?" Peter nodded, enlightened. He hadn't realized that his mother had been learned before she met Abelard; he had always assumed that it was as a result of being taught by him that she had become a scholar, and he'd often wondered how she had learnt so much so quickly. But then there was so much he hadn't known, hadn't understood – and still didn't.

"So it was hardly surprising that two such able, exceptional minds should also conceive an affection for one another – in body as well. Before long, that affection turned into a great love – and as a result, Heloise conceived a child." Porcarius glanced sideways at Peter but received no response. They were turning right at the riverside track in the direction of Great Bend, their progress slow, for it was dictated by Porcarius's pace. Peter just listened, with a curious blend of anticipation and dread, aware that his heart was beating at twice its usual speed.

"Well, the pregnancy had to be concealed from Heloise's uncle, of course, who was quite oblivious to what had been going on under his own roof, during the very lessons which he himself had begged Abelard to give his niece. For all his good looks, he had a reputation for abstinence, you see." Porcarius shook his head, admiring in retrospect his brother's audacity. "One night they disguised themselves as monks and rode here, to Le Pallet, where Heloise passed the time of her pregnancy." Turning back towards the manorhouse, now out of sight behind the angle of Boundary Ridge, he gestured vaguely: "And you already know the little room where you were born. It was just before Christmas in 1118 – I was here for the festival – and I remember it was a particularly cold, clear night, the sky was full of stars . . ."

59

"Go on, Uncle." Peter saw signs of the story slowing up. The next bit was what really mattered.

"Well, when you were a few months old, Abelard persuaded Heloise to return to Paris as his wife. I was back at my work in Angers at that time, but Denise told me afterwards how Heloise wept and begged him, with all the arguments she could think of, not to marry her – to persuade him that marriage would be their ruin. Prophetically, as it turned out."

"But why, I don't understand. The Church wouldn't have forbidden it, surely? *Why* didn't she want to marry him?"

"No, you're right. Abelard was not a priest in those days and he would have been allowed to marry."

By now they had almost reached Great Bend and the ford, much less boggy after all the fine weather. On the far side of the bend a fallen willow provided a convenient resting place – as sometimes before it had provided a convenient obstacle for jumping the ponies over. As they sat down, Peter noticed how breathless Porcarius had become.

"Then why was marriage likely to ruin them?" Peter had a sudden radiant vision of what his childhood at Le Pallet might have been like, surrounded by his own parents as well as by Denise and the other members of the family whom he loved.

"Heloise" – Porcarius found it difficult to refer to her as 'your mother' – "felt that marriage would damage Abelard's calling. It was a sort of moral ruin she feared, I think. You see, Abelard, though not a priest, aspired to be one of the very great Christian philosophers and theologians. And all the great spiritual heroes of the Christian Church have linked true learning and study of the Scriptures with a pure life and with celibacy. She felt that if he were married and formally bound to her in the flesh, he'd no longer be free to devote himself

60

to moral philosophy. Can you understand that?"

"No, not really."

In truth Porcarius, who had never had the opportunity to lose his celibacy, also found the reasoning quite hard to understand.

"Well, whether or not we understand it, it was something Heloise felt passionately. And Denise said she was dazzled when she heard Heloise rehearse the arguments. She was learned enough to invoke the great teachers of the past, pagan as well as Christian – St Jerome, Seneca, St Augustine – who supported her view. She knew they were all teachers whom Abelard deeply admired as well – but it was all to no avail."

"So in the end she gave in?"

"Yes, and they went back to Paris."

There was another pause. Although Porcarius had never loved a woman, he would have given a great deal to father a child, and deep in his heart he had never forgiven Abelard for deserting so completely his one and only son. And that Heloise could simply ride away, entrusting forever to another woman the baby she had seemed so rapturously happy to be carrying – and whose father she had finally agreed to marry – that he would never understand, not if he lived to be seventy. Perhaps that was partly why it had been such a long time before he or Denise had seriously tried to explain it all to Peter, for it was hard to explain something you didn't really understand yourself. He knew Denise shared his feelings, though loyalty to their brother had bound them to silence; over the years only an occasional well-timed glance or a shake of the head had conveyed their mutual agreement; as well as the special affection they both felt for the boy himself, their quiet, complicated, grey-eyed dreamer.

"And were married?" At last Peter's need to know as much as possible, everything, was becoming urgent: he no longer had any thought of sparing himself.

"Yes. Heloise's uncle – your great uncle, I suppose – was reconciled by Abelard's offer of marriage. He'd been outraged, of course, when they had escaped to Brittany and he found out what had been going on. But they kept the marriage secret."

"Secret. Why?" Peter frowned at the willow switch he was stripping with his nails.

"I can't be sure, but I think it was a sort of compromise. Perhaps they thought they could have the best of both worlds by keeping it secret: Abelard's high academic office, if not his spiritual purity, would be safe, and they would still have each other. But it gets complicated here: Abelard told me long after that Fulbert broke his promise of secrecy – he probably felt that if people knew about the marriage it would somehow make up for the dishonour that had been done to him as Heloise's guardian." Porcarius paused for breath; he was becoming quite tired. But he had got so far and knew he could not stop yet. Peter waited impatiently; two swans sailed by on the current and he thought how much he hated their hard, arrogant faces. He could never understand why they were considered beautiful. But then he often seemed to feel differently from other people. Perhaps, he reflected, that wasn't so surprising in view of all he was hearing now about his parents.

"Anyway, Heloise swore publicly that it was a lie, that no marriage had taken place, and I believe Fulbert then began to treat her very badly. So, to protect her, Abelard moved her to the convent at Argenteuil where she'd been brought up and educated by the nuns. When Fulbert found out where she was, he thought he'd been tricked again – he must have thought Abelard was getting rid of Heloise because he was tired of her." Porcarius paused for a moment. "And so he bribed one of Abelard's own servants to – well, I think you know what they did to him while he lay in bed in his lodgings."

They were silent again; Peter involuntarily put his hand over his private parts as if to protect them, for how could he help imagining the terrible scene. He did feel pity, in a remote, detached sort of way, but it was overlaid with physical revulsion at the barbaric act itself.

Porcarius misunderstood his silence and offered a little comfort:

"Strangely, you know, Abelard quite quickly came to accept what had happened. I think – I know – he genuinely believes it was a just punishment from God for the lustful way he had behaved. I've not seen him many times in the years between, but I've never heard him complain about the damage to his body. I think it was a far greater humiliation when he was forced to burn his book on the Holy Trinity – but that's another story." And it was indeed a singular thing, this almost humble acceptance by Abelard of his eunuch state – considering how he had never held back from violent criticism of those who treated him unfairly in other ways. Porcarius remembered his brother's words precisely: "The punishment came from God," he'd said, "as a father's rod, not a persecutor's sword." His body had been wounded, he believed, to heal his soul.

"And so what happened to my . . . to Heloise?"

"She took the veil at Argenteuil in obedience to your father's wishes."

A water-rat plopped out from its hole in the bank and disappeared among some rushes. The afternoon was turning cool; high wisps of cirrhus scribbled across a pale parchment sky and a new wind crumpled the surface of the river.

*She took the veil in obedience to your father's wishes*

63

*. . . in obedience to your father's wishes . . .* So much in so few words. This was the heart of it all, of course. She had given her life to God but not for God's sake; she had given it for the sake of the man she loved, but whom she thereby renounced forever, together with their only child. And because *he* wished it. How *could* he have made her do such a thing when it meant abandoning him, her baby son, *their* baby son?

He had heard enough now. The hurt welled up, hot, inside him, but nonetheless he shivered and said, "It's getting cold down here, let's go back."

"There's much more to tell you – about Abelard's trials and tribulations. Literally. But yes, sufficient unto the day . . . Perhaps he can tell you the rest himself."

At that moment Peter cared nothing for his father's trials. *In obedience to his wishes . . .* drummed in his head like a battle-song.

They walked back in silence, Porcarius struggling to keep up and wondering if he had said too much. He was anxious to tell Denise what had happened. But when they reached the drawbridge, Peter turned to him and said quietly, "Thank you, Uncle. Some of what you've told me I already knew, of course, but only in fragments. You've helped to put them together for me and I'm very obliged to you." It was a stiff, formal little speech, more like the way in which he was accustomed to talking to his Uncle Hugh than to Porcarius, but he did feel different, older somehow, as if a year or more had passed in the course of a single afternoon. And he no longer felt confused; he felt angry, but at least now he knew why.

# 6

Parting from Porcarius, who headed for the Great Hall and a much-needed beaker of cider, Peter went back to the chapel to collect his rebec. He shoved at the thick oak door with his shoulder, for he was not at all in a reverent frame of mind, and was surprised that it gave way readily, the lever not being in place. Once inside, he realized immediately that he was not alone. In the shadows beside the back bench, startled out of an attitude of devout prayer by his entrance, knelt Nicolette.

Peter stood transfixed, his shoulder still against the door, not sure whether to advance or retreat. The rebec was still in the little stone font where he had left it for safekeeping, its mother-of-pearl inlay gleaming in flickering candlelight shed from a wall-niche above.

"I – I'm sorry," he said, hoarsely. "I didn't know anyone was in here. I just came . . ."

But Nicolette rose to her feet and said, "Please – it is not for *me* to stop *you* coming into the chapel." There was a pause and then she nodded towards the rebec. "It's such a pretty instrument. I was looking at it – without touching, of course."

Peter was suspicious; was she, possibly, making fun of him? "Yes. It was a gift from Compostela." Then, cautiously, "Would you like to look at it properly?"

She seemed so interested and moved towards him with such eagerness that Peter was reassured.

"Come, I'll show you." And so they sat down side

by side on the bench just inside the door, and Peter placed the instrument in her lap. After a few moments, he asked timidly, "Do you often come here to pray?"

"No, not alone like this. But today I kept thinking of Mother – it's half a year to the day since she died." They were still speaking in whispers. Peter noticed how her dark braids glowed almost red in the candlelight. "And my poor grandfather – I have prayed to God and all the saints I've heard of, but I fear that he will never be himself again. Maud's mandrake tea hasn't helped either."

"It *is* very sad to see him so. Baudri was always so masterful, taking charge of work on the estate, especially when Uncle Hugh was away. I used to be quite frightened of him when I was a child!" He spoke more slowly than usual, choosing his words carefully as if they were little offerings to be laid at her feet.

"Yes, and when Master Charles leaves to study at Angers, as they say he will soon, I know they will have to find another steward. And then what will become of him? There *is* my sister, but I don't think she'd have much time for Grandfather now."

Peter didn't think so either, though he didn't say as much – Nicolette's elder sister had married the village miller, but the marriage had a reputation for being unhappy. A more buxom version of Nicolette, Constance – as she had most ironically been christened – was susceptible to the attentions of certain other men: Robert the big blacksmith had been mentioned; Louis had reported that piece of gossip back to the manorhouse but no one knew for sure.

Nicolette had turned her brown eyes on him; he noticed for the first time the birthmark, shaped like a tiny arrow-head, just above her left eyebrow, the long lashes which began to curl at the ends and – so closely were they huddled on the narrow bench – the soft down on her upper lip. Struggling against a desire to touch her cheek, to put his own lips to the birthmark and to the soft down, he said instead, quite matter-of-factly:

"But you must know that my uncle and aunt would never abandon him. His home is here, at the house – he's served them faithfully all these years . . ." He stopped, embarrassed that he'd just emphasized what divided them.

But she nodded, reassured, and seemed not at all perturbed by the reminder of her inferior social position. Why should she be, after all?

"It is the truth. Your family are good masters. He would not be so safe at Le Bourget, as I hear."

Nicolette was never sad for very long. After a short silence, during which Peter desperately sought something to talk about so as to prolong this blissful little interlude, she gave a chuckle. Peter darted a glance at her, afraid again that she might be laughing at him. But she was staring at the stone font in front of them.

"That devil. I think he's meant to look frightening, but he makes me laugh." Then, wondering if she'd sounded irreverent, she looked anxiously at him, her lower lip caught by several white teeth.

Peter smiled. He'd often had the same thought. They started talking about the other figures which struggled round the stone vessel, carved by a journeyman mason, who had stayed for two months at Le Pallet before Agnes's baptism four years ago. Peter told Nicolette how he had sat for hours exactly where she had just been praying, watching the man at his craft. His ambition had been to reach Autun and work there with the famous master sculptor, Gislebertus. "I'd like to go there one day too – Autun, Vezelay, and above all, Cluny."

"Cluny? What's at Cluny?"

For a moment Peter was stunned. Did she really not know what Cluny was? He scanned her face; no, no sign of mockery.

"Cluny is . . ." he frowned, trying to remember the words of the tutor he'd shared with Charles and Louis until the previous summer, when the man had left to enter a Cluniac monastery, ". . . is a magnificent abbey where thousands of monks can assemble all at once, so magnificent with its vaulting and its frescoes that an emperor could have built nothing finer, and the music in its services is the best in France."

Nicolette giggled.

"It sounds as if you've seen it already." Too late, Peter knew he'd begun to bore her. What could she care about some abbey church on the other side of France that she was never likely to visit? She handed him back the rebec and sprang to her feet, brushing the dust of the bench from her blue woollen dress.

"I must go. The children will be needing me. I seem to have been here for hours . . . But it was nice talking to you like this, Master Peter." She added more shyly, "Thank you." And almost before Peter was aware of it, she'd disappeared through the slightly open door. For some time afterwards he sat staring at the font, seeing the familiar carvings with new eyes, for an angel had just breathed fresh life into them.

Eventually he emerged from the dim light of the chapel and, with no destination consciously in mind but with Nicolette's shy words of thanks still in his ears, he made towards the gate. It wasn't until he heard his name called that he realized he'd been heading for 'his' apple-tree at the far end of the orchard. He stopped in his tracks, feeling a warm blush suffuse his face; after all, it wasn't really a very manly thing to do, to sit in an apple-tree considering one's feelings about the world.

It was Denise who had called him. Standing at the angle of the stone steps, which led upwards to the door of the Great Hall and downwards towards the kitchens, she was giving instructions to Berthe – thin, always starved-looking Berthe – who did most of the cooking at the manor. Porcarius had told her of his talk with Peter and she was anxious to see her nephew. She watched him approach with disquiet, then interest, then puzzlement. She'd expected him to be in the depths of one of his darkest moods, and had been anticipating a difficult time with him. But she was confounded by the distant, dreamy, and by no means unhappy expression on his face.

Bewildered, she thought to herself, perhaps after all I don't really understand him.

"Thank you, Berthe – that'll be all. Make the wheatear pies as you suggest for tomorrow."

When she and Peter were alone, Denise prompted gently, "Porcarius told me that he's talked to you."

Recognizing her concern, he touched her arm and said, "It's all right, Aunt Denise. Well, it's not all right, but what I mean is that Uncle Porcarius hasn't made it worse. In fact, there's a lot that he's made clearer for me. But there's still *so* much I don't understand." As he spoke, his dreamy expression vanished, and the familiar imploring one replaced it.

"Such as?" But she knew the answer full well.

"Why he had to keep the marriage secret when there was a child already born to it; why he made her take the veil; why she agreed; why he has only been to see me once in fifteen years: why I've never received one word from her who is – who *was* – my mother."

Denise would have liked to take him in her arms as she had when he hurt himself as a little boy, but in his new, maturer, angry questioning there was something that held her at a distance. He was bigger than her now

69

as well; he was, indeed, almost a man. With all her heart she would have answered him, if she could. But how could she, she whose devotion to her children and her foster-child – even to Louis, who had always needed her less than the others – was the bedrock of her existence? And to tell him that she had often pondered these things without finding a solution, that would surely hurt him even more, for he was searching so desperately for an explanation that could help him forgive.

This was a scene she had dreaded for fifteen years, though she'd never imagined that it would take place standing up, in the open courtyard.

But all she could say, after so many years of preparation, was:

"I think, one day, my Peter, you *will* understand. When you are truly a man." She could only pray that this would turn out to be the case.

" 'My' Peter. That's the heart of it, isn't it? I'm more yours than ever I was theirs." He didn't know why he said it or what he really meant by it. When she flinched he bitterly regretted the words; he hadn't wanted to be ungrateful, but now he wasn't sure how to unsay it. His eyes were charcoal-grey in a face pinched and white with resentment.

But Denise ignored it, and went on, "There is one thing I can put right. Abelard has actually been to see you twice. There's the time when you were a little boy of seven, which you've told me you hardly remember. That was on the way to be abbot at that dreadful place, St Gildas. But he came again in the spring of 1131. It was after he'd been to install Heloise at the Paraclete near Provins – the place he'd retreated to with Thibault after he was wounded. His students had all followed him and built a settlement and a chapel, so they could continue to be taught by him. Heloise and the other nuns had been expelled from their convent at Argenteuil – I don't know why, I can't tell you that. Anyway, he gave them the Paraclete and stayed there for a while helping them to settle in, and then went to see the Pope consecrating a high altar somewhere – Morigny, I think, but it doesn't really matter – and on his way back to St Gildas, he came here, with the purpose of seeing you."

"So why *didn't* I see him?"

"You were away on the other side of Poitiers with Hugh's family. You remember the time?"

Peter ignored the query. "And you *never* told me," he accused.

"No. I was afraid to. It seemed so cruel." There were tears in her eyes as she looked up at him – he was now a good head taller than her. To begin with they had spoken in whispers to avoid being overheard by any servants hovering at the open door of the kitchen below; then their voices had become normal, and now, forgetting where they stood, Denise's apology became impassioned.

"I'm sorry, Peter. It caused me many a sleepless hour, as God is my witness. But how *could* I tell you that the one time you have ever been away from Le Pallet for more than a few days was the moment when your father chose to visit you? It was totally unexpected. I didn't know whether to be pleased or sorry to see him, though it was only the second time since 'it' happened – and I should have given him a better welcome." She shook her head, aware with relief that Peter's face was less accusing.

After all, he thought, what did it really matter? Two visits in fifteen years didn't make a father, and next week, in just eight days, he'd have his chance to challenge this man they all seemed to think was so special.

"The whole wretched thing is like a story invented

by a witch – ill-luck at every turn." She sighed.

"Was it bad luck when I was born? A bad child – leading to Abelard's punishment from God?"

"How can you even *think* to ask that? *Peter!*" To Denise the question was so ludicrous that she failed to take it seriously. "Come – we should go inside now."

Well, at least he now understood what those two merchants had referred to, five years before in the Great Hall, when they'd talked of renewed gossip about Abelard and Heloise. It must have been while he was helping her and the nuns make a new home at the Paraclete. He could at least forgive them that. He had wondered sometimes whether the remark meant that they'd after all lived together as man and wife, without him.

At the far end of the Great Hall, Porcarius was helping Hugh and Charles with some document or other – probably the rent ledger, for collecting rent was one of Porcarius's chief duties as administrator for the cathedral chapter at Angers and he understood such things well. Louis, astride a stool, his long legs stretched out on either side, was playing draughts with Ralph. Baudri was on his knees near the fire, frantically searching for something in the rushes. "Lady Lucie's lost her ring, Lady Lucie's lost her ring," he was mumbling to himself, distressed anew by a loss which had happened well over twenty years before, when Denise's mother Lucie had indeed lost a precious ring. Louis took advantage of their arrival to bring the game to an end.

"Ah! That means dinner will be up soon, I expect. Anyway, you're too slow, Ralph – I get really bored playing with you." He stretched himself luxuriously, got up and whistled at two of the hounds who were snarling at each other over a bone. Charles overheard and called out, "You're no good at draughts anyway,

Louis. You just don't want to be beaten by Ralph."

Ralph grinned with pleasure – for in truth he *was* slow – and then, seeing Peter, cried, "Good, come on Peter. You'll play, won't you?"

But Peter suddenly felt overwhelmingly tired. It had, after all, been one of the most momentous afternoons of his life.

"I'm sorry, Ralph. I don't feel like draughts now. Perhaps later. And I don't want dinner tonight, Aunt Denise." Not waiting for an answer, he pulled back the leather curtain in the corner and slowly climbed the spiral staircase – each step at a time for once, unusual for any of the boys – to his tiny turret bedchamber. He was followed only by the frowning glances of Denise and Porcarius, whose eyes had met in mutual unease.

## 7

Fortunately for Peter the week that followed was a season of great activity on the manor. The weather, reflecting his state of mind, became mixed and changeable: low grey clouds marbled the sky and threatened worse to come, but here and there they shifted to reveal ragged patches of purest egg-shell blue.

Lambert, the ploughman, was now permanently out of action for gangrene had spread from his foot. Despite the efforts of the parish priest, who made daily visits to his hut to sprinkle consecrated water on the stinking wound, there was little more that could be done for him save an amputation, which he was resolutely resisting. Sir Hugh also made dutiful visits to the sick man, but it was no hardship for him to take a turn with the autumn ploughing, for he had always loved working on the land. Louis helped him with the ox-team, while Charles and Peter and Ralph and most of the villagers busied themselves with the grape harvest.

Most of the vineyards were at the opposite end of the estate from the manor-house, on the south-facing slopes beyond the mill on Little Bend. A wooden bridge crossed the river to give access to them, just before the large triangular piece of Lammas land which formed the western end of Le Pallet. To begin with Peter and Ralph worked as a pair, Peter cutting off the bunches of grapes with his bill-hook and throwing them into the deep basket attached to

Ralph's back. But Ralph soon grew tired of trudging, heavily laden, down to the huge wooden vats at the foot of the slope, in which the grapes were being trodden by two peasants in each vat. Knowing how clumsy he was, Peter refused to let him have a turn with the bill-hook, and so, after a grumble, he wandered off in the hope of having a turn at the treading. Soon Peter was joined by Fulk and Guy, big Fulk effortlessly carrying the basket, which Guy and Peter had quickly filled, down to the vats. It was back-punishing work, but Peter rejoiced in the hard physical labour for it stopped him thinking too much. Until, that is, Guy began to tease his elder brother.

"Hurry up next time with the basket, Fulk. You're loitering down there – just because it's big-bosomed Madeleine in the nearest vat. I saw you. Nicolette wouldn't like that at all – and Peter here could give you away when he goes back up to the house."

Peter felt his throat contract and go dry. What was this? What had Fulk to do with Nicolette?

"What do you mean?" he asked, too abruptly. He straightened up, wincing, ostensibly, at the ache in his lower back.

"Didn't you know?" laughed Guy. "Nicolette's been promised to Fulk since they were about six or seven years old. Not that she's much of a catch now, with both parents dead. Still, Father's not worried about that – and she's as pretty a wench as any between here and Nantes. When are the banns going to be read then, Fulk?"

Fulk blushed. "Not yet awhile. I want to travel a bit more. Got a taste for it on that journey to Compostela. Time enough for marriage after I'm twenty, I reckon."

Guy laughed again, and dangled a bunch of grapes into his mouth. "You're just waiting for her to ripen a bit more – isn't he, Peter? I shouldn't wait too long –

she might split open and go mouldy. Like . . . so!" And he picked off a grape which had done just that and threw it playfully at his brother's face.

Peter, heavy-hearted, was back on his knees, busier than ever with the bill-hook. It had rained during the night and the smell of damp earth and ripe fruit made him feel faintly sick. Again and again he tried to comfort himself with the last words she had spoken to him: "It was nice talking to you like this, Master Peter – thank you." *Perhaps* everything was not yet lost.

It rained again the day Abelard and Raoul were expected. It was raining at first light and it didn't stop all day, so there could be no work outside to distract. Instead, Peter passed the time restlessly playing half a game of chess with Ralph – who seldom concentrated for the length of a whole game in any case – studying a piece of Latin verse with Charles and Porcarius and trying to play his new rebec. He also visited Peggy in the stable – mainly to annoy Thomas – and then the hawks, who were kept in a small but separate part of the stable sheds, in order to annoy Raymond, the falconer. Ralph, as a small boy, had once told Raymond that he looked like one of his goshawks. Ralph was chased out of the building, but had been lucky to escape so lightly. It had been the spontaneous, unmalicious observation of a small child, and as such had been deadly accurate; Charles, Louis and Peter, who had all been there, dared not look at each other for fear of collapsing with laughter. Louis, who, as Peter well knew, was not usually so reluctant to make fun of others, had always been at pains to please Raymond, even at that age of about nine, for he was passionate about hawking and loved to help him train the birds. As Peter dawdled now in front of one of the mews, making faces at an eyass – a hawk which Louis had taken in the summer as a fledgling from its nest – he reflected that his own lack of interest in the sport was probably in direct proportion to Louis's passion for it.

By the early afternoon Peter could stand the idleness and suspense no longer. Ignoring Thomas's grumbles ("This'm no weather for joy-riding"), he bridled Peggy and rode out into the rain. They would be coming from Nantes in the late afternoon or early evening, according to Raoul's message, so Peter set off towards Great Bend and the bridleway over Boundary Ridge. Peggy made her displeasure very clear by tossing her neck even more than usual, and by stopping several times to bury her muzzle in the now soggy overgrown water meadow. It was usually a good hour's ride over the ridge and down to the beech and sycamore woods which bordered the road from Nantes, but because of the conditions today, it took them at least an hour and a half.

Peter had no particular plan worked out in his mind. It wasn't that he intended to spy on his father, but he did have a vague notion that at least if he saw what Abelard looked like, it would somehow help when they later came face to face. And anyway, he had to do something to pass the time. So he and Peggy entered the woods and ambled along parallel with the road, but at such a distance as to be more or less invisible from it. The rain, filtered by the branches overhead, dripped and spat in eerie accompaniment to the dull thud of Peggy's hooves on the woodland floor, which was fast becoming a damp compost of leaves and nuts, sorrel and nettle. Once they startled some deer who abruptly abandoned their meal of bark and melted into the mottled interior of the forest. Peter rode up and down for a while before eventually coming to a halt near where the road branched off up the hill to become the bridleway to Le Pallet. Sitting there feeling increasingly miserable and wet, he drew his cloak more tightly round his shoulders and his hood more closely into his face. At that moment he realized that when Abelard did eventually pass he would almost certainly be hidden in the folds of his own cloak and hood. Why hadn't he thought of that before?

"Peggy, you were right all along," he said, patting her damp grey neck.

It was then that he heard the unmistakable sounds of approaching riders; hoof thuds, harness jingles, voices. The noises grew louder; Peggy pricked one ear and for a moment Peter was terrified that she might give a welcoming neigh and betray him. But she didn't let him down, and presently he saw the little party pass just about a hundred feet from where he stood concealed. Two mules ridden by servants followed the horses, one a large piebald which Peter recognized as his Uncle Raoul's usual mount. On the far side – avoiding the deep, flooded cart-tracks in the middle – rode a man in a brown cloak, much larger than Raoul, on a dark bay palfrey. As they turned off up towards the ridge, the larger man, to Peter's surprise, threw back his head and gave a hearty laugh. As he did so his hood fell back far enough to reveal a fringe of grey-white hair. Peter recognized Raoul's quieter laugh as they shared some joke – and then they had passed.

Strange, Peter reflected, that of all the ways in which he had imagined his father – lecturing to eager crowds of students, reading and writing hunched over a candle late into the night, haranguing the sinful monks at St Gildas, writhing in agony after his mutilation, yes, even making passionate love to Heloise – he had never once thought of him as, quite simply, laughing at a joke. In truth, laughter did not come easily to Abelard, and less so now than ever. That he did so with such heartiness at that moment was a measure of his relief to have at last left behind him the danger and distress of life at St Gildas, and to be on this rare visit to the familiar, much loved valley of his childhood.

Strange, too, that Peter had never pictured him with grey hair, though at fifty-five it was only to be expected. But strangest of all, perhaps, was that he *felt* nothing at that moment – except very wet.

He allowed some twenty minutes to pass before following the party back up towards Boundary Ridge and the manor. Peggy's pace quickened as she realized that they were homeward bound, and once or twice he had to restrain her, for it wouldn't have done to catch them up. When he reached his favourite vantage point above Great Bend, hidden in its willows, he thought suddenly that it would seem strange to everyone that he was not at the house to welcome the visitors. Hugh and Denise would probably see it as a mark of disrespect, and be angry with him. It occurred to him that it might also cause offence to Abelard himself. So now he urged the pony on, already working out a plan for getting into the house unseen – it wouldn't be the first time he'd stood on Peggy's back and hauled himself up onto the steep stable roof which overlapped the courtyard wall in one place. From there he could drop down into the narrow alleyway between the stable and the wall, and into the house via a little side door in the South Tower. This door only led down to the servants' sleeping-quarters and the kitchens, but from there an internal stairway gave access to the Hall. Not a very fitting or dignified way to receive such a long-awaited guest – but if he hurried he might just be able to give the impression he'd been there all the time, and he was still child enough to find some appeal in the plan.

But at the point where the riverside track branched

off towards the orchards and the house, Peter was unexpectedly accosted. Philippe, Raymond's slow-witted nephew, emerged as if from nowhere and ran alongside Peggy, obviously extremely agitated. He kept pointing into the distance in the direction of Maud's hut and the mill on Little Bend, shaking his head and squeaking, desperately trying to make Peter understand something. Peter noticed that one of his round, too-close-together eyes was discoloured, and he thought indignantly of beak-nosed Raymond, who had patience only for his birds.

"I really feel something should be done about that poor child, idiot or not," Denise had once said in Peter's hearing to Hugh.

"It's nothing to do with us, my love. He's fortunate at least to have food and shelter. Raymond could have left him to die," Hugh had replied, who, with his own children, had made unusually little use of the rod as a punishment.

But now, Philippe's wretchedness seemed to have nothing to do with his eye injury. Peter had never seen him in such a state. Bewildered, he leant down and hauled the blabbering child up onto the pony in front of him. Normally this would have resulted in a happy smile; today it did nothing to stop the head-shaking and pointing and squeaking.

The branch in the track made Peter's dilemma painfully clear. Either he investigated the cause of Philippe's distress and kept Abelard waiting, or he returned immediately to the manor-house with the child, whose condition made any hope of a secret entry unthinkable – and at such a time who would there be to pay any attention to the agitated boy? Certainly not Raymond. Peter didn't consider for long. He was no hero, but neither was he one to ignore easily another's cry for help. Abelard could wait; after all, had he not made

Peter wait long enough? And there was a nice irony in the thought of one of the greatest scholars in France taking his turn after the village idiot.

The rain had at last begun to ease off, but Peggy tossed her head in disgust at the command to make this last-minute detour. Seeing that Peter was now taking him seriously, Philippe became calmer. But he watched the river intently as they trotted past the strip-fields, past Maud's plot of land and on towards Little Bend and the mill. When the mill came into sight, he again became agitated and began to gesticulate. For a few moments Peter still couldn't see what was causing so much excitement. But then he saw.

Floating head-down, about thirty feet from the mill wheel, the wide bodice of his tunic caught as if impaled by the rushes, his feet half-buried in the muddy shallows, was an unmistakable figure. Old Baudri, steward at Le Pallet for more than two generations and Nicolette's much loved grandfather, lay drowned.

# 8

Peter's heart lurched at the pitiful sight, and then his mind began to race. What should he do? Who should he tell first? Should he go back to the house? Or fetch the priest? Should he leave Philippe to guard the body? Or should he himself try to drag it out of the water? In his shock, he had absent-mindedly begun to stroke Philippe's hair, which seemed to have a calming effect on the boy. His mind began to clear. Of course he couldn't leave Philippe alone, and it would be madness to try to drag the waterlogged body out of the river by himself. He must go for help, and to whoever was nearest at hand. Of course – Henri the miller, married to flighty Constance and therefore Baudri's grandson-in-law, was the obvious person. He was strong and thickset, too, he'd be able to help.

But just as Peter was about to turn back towards the mill, he caught sight of Guillaume of the Grapes who had appeared in the vineyards on the other side of the river. He was leaning on a pole – the type all the peasants used to balance themselves when laden with the back-baskets – and was sadly inspecting the damage done to the harvest by the untimely rain.

"Guillaume, Guillaume, come over here," shouted Peter, and the sudden noise startled Philippe into renewed whimperings. When Guillaume had obediently crossed the wooden bridge, Peter dismounted and took Guillaume's arm:

"Look – down there!"

Guillaume looked and Peter saw him go a strange, ashen colour. He put his free hand on Peter's shoulder, who understood intuitively that the sight had brought back that other drowning of long ago, which had so tragically affected his life. More gently, but firmly, Peter said:

"Guillaume, we must get help. Please go to the mill and tell Henri and Constance, and I'll go back and alert them at the house as quickly as possible." Now that he had shared the discovery with someone else he immediately felt not only more in control, but also a renewed urgency to get back to the manor-house, where Abelard would even now be waiting for him. For Abelard was *here*, at Le Pallet! He repeated the words to himself as he rode away, and luxuriated in the blend of satisfaction and alarm which they gave him.

And meeting his father was not the only prospect to fill him with a conflict of feelings. For Nicolette must, of course, be told about her grandfather, and that task he would make sure to keep for himself. Peggy refused to do more than trot with Philippe's extra weight on her back, and all the slow way home two alternating vision-dreams whirled around Peter's head. In the one he was kneeling at the feet of the large brown-cloaked figure he'd glimpsed in the rain who, after telling him gently to rise, clasped him to his bosom as befitted the greeting of a long-lost son. In the other, a pale heart-shaped face, with no longer laughing eyes, rested on his shoulder while he, Peter, tightly enfolded its owner in a comforting embrace.

It was thus, under the circumstances, in a state of not altogether seemly excitement, that Peter clattered into the courtyard, and hurriedly left both Peggy and Philippe to the care – or in Philippe's case, the con-tempt – of one of Lambert's sons.

But as he entered the Great Hall, the first of the vision-dreams crumbled instantly away. In a blur Peter registered most of the adult members of his family grouped around the fire; but it was Hugh, not Abelard, who rose to confront – rather than meet – him. White-faced and thin-lipped he towered above Peter, who dropped humbly to his knees.

"We have been awaiting your pleasure. It is a great discourtesy that you have shown," he said icily, through clenched teeth, so that the others might not hear.

Everyone in the room was related to Peter, and most of them loved him, yet for a long moment he felt surrounded by enemies. No one tried to make the ordeal easier for him. The truth of the matter was that no one knew how to, but Peter couldn't know that; his heart was racing yet his chin tilted in a tiny gesture of defiance. If that's how they wanted it he'd show them he was equal to the occasion, just as young knights had to be equal to their initiation rites. With a dignity that could not fail to impress everyone watching, he announced, clearly and formally:

"I am sorry, Uncle, for my delay and I regret the discourtesy. None was intended. But," and here he very slightly rearranged the truth, "it was beyond my control, for I bear bad news – I have just discovered the body of Baudri, drowned in the river below the mill race."

The little thrill which gives a moment of pride to bearers of news, good and bad alike, enabled him then to survey the reaction of the group by the fire. The tall stranger in the brown cloak occupied the finest carved chair. He was watching Peter intently, but gave him no sign of acknowledgement. His only movement was the continuous gentle massaging of his neck with the fingers of his left hand, his left elbow resting on the arm of the huge oak chair. Peter had a vague sense of being reminded of someone else. Abelard did not seem to share in the looks of dismay which Raoul, Porcarius and Denise all exchanged, nor did he make the sign of the cross as Denise did. Baudri had of late become crazed with age, yet for all that they had never known a time when he wasn't there. For the three brothers and their sister it was sad news indeed. Abelard, without taking his eyes off Peter's face, expressed what was in all their minds:

"So - poor Baudri. Our childhood finally breathes its last with him. How fitting that Raoul and I should be here."

"Not quite its last, Abelard. There's still old Thomas in the stables - but I think he will see us all on our way!" Then Porcarius came to his nephew's rescue, "Rise, Sir Peter!"

"Yes, yes - very well, Peter, you had good reason to be late. But we could not have known that," acknowledged Hugh, a little grudgingly but trying, as always, to be fair-minded. And, as Peter rose from his knees, they heard through the door, which he'd left open in his haste, the tolling of the church bell down in the village.

"I'd better go and see that the body is brought up here to our chapel," said Hugh, who bowed towards the visitors and excused himself.

Louis jumped up: "I'll go with you - to help." Because of the rain he'd been sitting inside all day, which was very unusual for Louis, and he was impatient for action, any action. He quite resented the fact that it was Peter who had had the excitement of discovering Baudri's body. Denise, thinking of some other instructions, followed them.

Peter stood there, not knowing what to do next. Again, none of the adults seemed willing or able to help him. He felt Abelard's gaze on him again, yet

85

dared not meet his eyes.

It was Ralph who broke the ice. Sitting in his favourite position, knees hunched up to his chin and far too close to the fire, as he was always being told, he had been looking steadily and suspiciously at Abelard for some time. He had met him during his last visit to Le Pallet, three and a half years before, but no one had told him then who the visitor was for fear that he would repeat it when Peter returned from Poitiers. Now he said in his childish forthright way – for his ways were still those of a nine-year-old, although he would be thirteen next spring – "Are you really Peter's father, sir? You don't look at all like him."

No one could help smiling and the tension lessened immediately. It somehow made it possible for Peter to look straight at Abelard and to bow cautiously.

In a surprisingly sonorous voice, Abelard answered, "As for that, Ralph, you don't resemble in the slightest either your father or your mother! But yes, I am Peter's father." He said this last without a trace of emotion. But now he spoke to Peter for the first time: "Come here, child, and let me see how you *do* look."

Peter walked meekly to the chair and once again dropped to his knee; this, at last, was a little more like his vision-dream. But it was the only part that was to come true.

"No, don't kneel – sit here beside me." Charles, who had already made himself comfortable in the rushes at Abelard's feet, basking in a position which he knew would have been the envy of hundreds of aspiring scholars, moved a little to make way for his cousin. Abelard's attention turned for a moment to Porcarius, who had got up to replenish everyone's beakers of cider.

Peter, now in a position to scrutinize him, was surprised by how manly and handsome Abelard still was.

86

Neither age nor life's ravages had dimmed the brightness of his dark eyes, whose near blackness was accentuated by thick grey-white eyebrows and only slightly receding hair. His teeth were still unusually even and white. He was the sort of man you felt compelled to look at again and again; and, as Peter did look again, he knew who it was that his father reminded him of. There was no mistaking the cruel likeness. Abelard's particular type of dark, flashing, emphatic good looks had been passed on not to his fairer, fine-boned son but to his second nephew, to Louis.

Realizing this, Peter now took his eyes away from Abelard's face without difficulty. To his aunt, who had returned to the group and was looking at him apprehensively, he said, "Aunt Denise, I feel I should find Nicolette and tell her what's befallen her grandfather." He had been expecting her to appear with the children at any moment, for dinner was already being set out at the end of the Hall, but there was no sign of her.

"That's kind of you, Peter, but Nicolette will certainly know by now. Berthe told her Baudri hadn't been seen since this morning, so she went out just before our visitors arrived to see if he was at the mill with Constance."

So Nicolette had been just feet away all the time, unsuspecting. And he had asked – no, instructed – *Guillaume* to go to the mill with the news. So much for that blissful vision of a comforting embrace . . .

But perhaps this was only right and just. For hadn't he come close to regarding Baudri's death simply as an excuse for indulging this glorious new desire of his? He remembered what Porcarius had said, about Abelard accepting the terrible thing that had been done to his body as just reward for his lustful behaviour. This might be just a tiny thing in comparison, but it brought him a little nearer to understanding his father's forbearance.

Denise was now asking Abelard:

"Brother, I don't know how long it was in your mind to stay, but it would be an excellent thing if you could take Baudri's burial service."

Porcarius and Raoul nodded in agreement. "Yes indeed. That would be what our dear father Berengar would have wanted," said Raoul, quietly, looking into the fire.

Abelard smiled at Denise. She was fifteen years younger than he and, almost forty and mother of five though she was, she would always be his 'little sister'.

"It seems decided then. When have I not heeded your instructions?" Sitting back in the throne-like chair, it was apparent that he was beginning to relax. For Abelard, the estate and its house at Le Pallet were a haven in a hostile world; for the first time in years he was enjoying the company of those he knew and trusted best in the world – save for one – and contemplating a meal which no one would have tried to poison. But, at fifty-five and no longer in the best of health – Peter couldn't help noticing how the hand which held the beaker shook, so that it had to be laid for support on the arm of the chair – there was still so much to do, and he could not afford to linger. He would bury Baudri certainly, and then hasten back to Paris to resume his teaching and his writing. He had been away from it for far too long during those desolate, seemingly wasted years at St Gildas.

As they moved away from the fire to take their places at table, Denise seemed to read his thoughts.

"You must be pleased to be back at Le Pallet, brother? They've been bad years for you, I think."

"Indeed they have. In fact, sister, we must speak

quietly with one another before I leave." He had already lowered his voice, and Peter pretended not to be listening. "I have written down the story of all my misfortunes – not just as abbot of St Gildas you understand – and I want to leave a copy here, together with some letters, where I know they will be safe for posterity." For Abelard there was no doubt that future generations would have an interest in his story.

"Of course." No more was said then, but Peter's curiosity was aroused. Correspondence. With whom? With his mother Heloise perhaps? If so, such correspondence would be bound to concern him. Perhaps some of it was actually intended *for* him. It seemed that at last he was on the threshold of understanding what had driven his parents to turn their backs on him. For the first time he looked forward to this new understanding with eager anticipation, not with anger or dread. Perhaps that was the effect of seeing his father in person – his flashing eyes, his whitening hair, his shaking hand . . .

"Thérèse's geese are impossible to beat. I've not had better with the Bishop," claimed Porcarius, greedily stripping a leg with the grease running down his chin. For a moment Abelard stopped eating: perhaps he was remembering that in the months which Heloise had spent at Le Pallet she used to love to help Thérèse bring in the geese and ducks at night, so that they didn't lay their eggs in the marshy ground by the river. Country life had been a novelty to her, brought up as she had been in a convent near Paris and then in the cloisters of Notre Dame itself.

"She cooks better than Berthe too, but we daren't say so." Thérèse was Berthe's sister, and Berthe only ever allowed her to help in the kitchens, and then grudgingly, when her own poultry was on the table at the manor-house.

As Porcarius reached for another helping, Abelard observed, "I see your ways haven't changed, Porcarius. Take care though – remember what the famous doctor Gregory of Nazianzus said, about the beast which is our body being violent and demanding enough without feeding it extra rich or lavish food!"

"Nonsense! The Lord himself said that man is not defiled by what goes into his mouth but by what comes out of it!"

Without hesitation, Abelard countered:

"But what about 'Take heed to yourselves lest at any time your hearts be overcharged with surfeiting and drunkenness'?"

" 'Behold, how good and how pleasant it is for brethren to dwell together in unity'."

This quotation from the Psalms was a quiet contribution from Raoul. It made them all laugh, and Denise, flushed and happy, beamed down the table at them all, savouring the moments of rare family reunion. To show he had meant no real offence, Abelard took the cider flagon and replenished Porcarius's earthenware beaker. Then, raising his own, he said, "To our dear parents, Berengar and Lucie, and to our brother Dagobert – God rest their souls!"

Hugh returned to the Hall during this second welcome feast in just over a week, but it wasn't until they were almost finished that Louis came back, hurriedly and rather flushed. He exchanged a few whispered words with his mother, who rose and excused herself.

"Nicolette is back. I think I should go and speak to her," she explained.

Louis didn't offer an explanation but followed his mother back out of the Hall without a glance at the family around the table. Peter watched him go and guessed, with the certainty of love's imagination, what had happened.

# 9

It was the following morning before Peter saw
Nicolette again. Denise had tactfully suggested that he
and Charles should take Abelard out for a nostalgic
ride around the estate. On his way to the stables to
prepare the horses, he came upon a touching scene by
the well: Agnes, sobbing violently, was being comforted by Nicolette, who crouched before the child,
holding her hands and looking earnestly into her face.

"Berthe didn't really mean it, Agnes."

"Yes she did, I know she did."

"I don't know what you're making such a fuss
about. It's only a dog – you're *silly*, Agnes." This was
Agatha's considered opinion, as she played with two
wooden dolls on the wide stone edge of the well.

At that moment Nicolette caught sight of Peter.

"Oh Master Peter," she called in relief, "I can't do
anything with Agnes. Berthe threatened to put the runt
of Blanche's litter in the stewpot and Agnes is convinced she meant it."

"Please can I keep her, Peter?" wailed Agnes, looking
up at him with soft brown eyes just like her mother's.

Peter bent down and picked up the little girl. "I
haven't seen the puppy, Agnes, but if it's very tiny it
won't survive anyway. There's really no point . . ."

Nicolette shook her head and exchanged a knowing
smile with Peter. She looked lovelier than ever in her
black mourning dress, he thought: paler, more fragile
and somehow older.

"I'm really sorry about Baudri," he said quietly. He had been wondering how he could broach the subject but the moment, when it came, was much easier than he'd expected.

Agnes stopped crying and looked at him. "Baudri's *dead*," she told him earnestly.

"Yes, Agnes, I know."

"It was you who found him," Nicolette stated simply. And, as if that discovery could somehow have given him extra insight, she asked, "Do you think his soul was pure when he drowned? I fear that his mind wasn't sound enough to repent at the last. But I pray that he did. Please pray for that too, Master Peter." She looked at him so plaintively that Peter felt as if something at his very centre was dissolving.

"I shall pray for his soul, indeed. But I'm sure that in his lucid moments he was able to repent. God wouldn't punish him for his sick mind."

"I hope you're right," she said dubiously. "But sometimes I can't help the thought that the sickness he had was already a punishment from God – perhaps for some sin he committed when he was young."

"Father says everyone who does wicked things will be punished by God one day," offered Agatha unhelpfully. One of her dolls fell over perilously near the inner edge of the well surround. "Naughty Ralph, that's very dangerous," she exclaimed, slapping the wooden figure surprisingly hard on its leg.

Peter and Nicolette began to walk towards the stables. Peter was, as before in the chapel, desperately trying to think of something to say that would prolong the conversation. Suddenly, they both became aware that Agnes was walking between them, holding each by the hand. Peter, blushing, immediately let go, but with a little rush of joy he wondered if the moment had been some sort of omen.

"Can I have a ride?" asked Agnes, and Agatha, never one to be left out, caught them up and added, "Me, too, *please* Peter."

"No, not today. I have to take – our visitor – out around the manor." In her disappointment Agnes suddenly remembered the doomed puppy.

"What about Blanche's puppy? Peter, tell Berthe she can't cook him," she wailed.

"Agnes, no one wants to eat dog for dinner, I assure you. They'll get rid of her, I'm afraid, but not in a boiling pot. She won't feel anything. It'll probably be a quick drowning in the river."

The blood drained from his face as he realized what he'd said. He could have bitten right through his tongue. Nicolette lowered her head.

"Nicolette, I'm so sorry – I didn't think . . . I . . ." He floundered, helpless.

When she looked up her expression was one he couldn't interpret. But when she said quietly, "It's all right," there was, to his overwhelming relief, a hint of the old laughter in her eyes.

"Agnes," Peter said firmly to the little girl, "go and tell Berthe to do nothing with that puppy until I get back. I must go now." To Nicolette he said no more, but his grey eyes proclaimed the clearest message.

Thomas wouldn't hear of Peter preparing Abelard's palfrey – Peter thought he'd never seen the old chap so eager to work, or so chatty.

"Where are the boys today?"

"Down with their poor father. He'm following old Baudri in a few days, no mistake. I'm better off without them, to tell you'm the truth, Master Peter."

One month, even two weeks earlier, Peter could never have believed that he would so soon be riding around Le Pallet in the company of his father, and, even more amazing, that Abelard would not command his entire attention. As Charles eagerly took the opportunity to ask Abelard's advice on his own future, Peter repeated to himself again and again his tactless gaffe and pictured Nicolette's strange expression – a blend of pain, surprise and amusement. He imagined the different ways in which Louis – in stark contrast – might have broken the news to her the previous evening, no doubt offering smooth, comforting, well-chosen words: the possibilities became increasingly florid, until he had Louis leaping from his horse in his agile way to lift her from the ground and enfold her in his arms. So livid with jealousy did Peter's fantasy become that it completely failed to take account of the decorum which the situation would have demanded. But not once did he wonder how Fulk would console his betrothed; it was Louis alone who was the object of his dread.

It was hardly surprising, then, that as they rode across Cow Common, the proud straight figure and handsome profile on the palfrey beside him were contaminated by their resemblance to Louis. It was not an auspicious start to this his first – and maybe his last – dialogue with the father he had for so long yearned to meet. And Porcarius's words returned to accompany the thud of the horses' hooves: *She took the veil in obedience to his wishes, in obedience to his wishes . . .*

"So you'd advise me to choose Chartres, although it's so much further than Nantes or Angers?" Charles was saying thoughtfully.

"Yes, Charles, I would. You could not receive a better grounding than at Chartres. Raoul tells me that you have the makings of a good scholar, so it's important that you have excellent teachers from the start. Maybe the ones at Chartres are not as famous today as certain others I could name, who have made reputations for themselves in other schools, but remember, both of you – " and he included Peter now with his glance, "– there is an abundance of words where there is no abundance of meaning. *Copia verborum est, ubi non est copia sensus. Fructu, non foliis pomorum quisque cibatur.* We take nourishment from the fruit of trees, not the leaves; the meaning is more important than the words which convey it."

Charles gazed at his distinguished uncle with undisguised admiration though not really understanding what – or whom – he was getting at in all this. It was in Paris, where he knew Abelard was bound, that he really wanted to study. Abelard seemed to read his thoughts:

"Yes, you'll find the great Fulbert's liberal spirit still alive at Chartres – though he died over a hundred years ago. Then, later, you could come on to Paris, where I hope to be teaching again. But first you must climb onto the shoulders of the ancient philosophers in order to see just a little further than they. For that's how we modern scholars are, you know – as dwarfs on the shoulders of giants. And it was Bernard of Chartres who said that; yes, Charles, I would like my father's eldest grandson to head for Chartres. My father Berengar had a great love of learning and he would have approved."

Charles nodded in satisfaction. "Yes, I have quite clear memories of him reading to me from the Scriptures when I was very small. And of course I bear his name – Charles Berengar – after both my grandfathers."

As they embarked on the track leading from Cow Common along the bottom of the wooded incline which rose towards the boundary with Le Bourget, they passed Thérèse, two wooden buckets of milk suspended from a yoke across her shoulders.

"The geese were excellent," called Charles. Like his father, Hugh, Charles took an interest in the individual

95

peasants on the estate.

"Thank you, Master Charles." She looked curiously and shyly at the visitor, who remained silent. "They're always best at this time of year after getting at the stubble."

"But yours are better than most."

"Is *that* Thérèse?" said Abelard, as they rode on. "I remember her as a baby – they didn't think she'd live. It was her mother who cooked for our parents, that's how I remember."

Abelard now turned his gaze on Peter, who rode in silence beside him.

"It seems to me, Astralabe, that Chartres would be a suitable place of learning for you too in a year or so's time – because of your name if for no other obvious reason! It was at Chartres that the astrolabe – an Arabic instrument – first became known and understood in France."

Peter tried rather unsuccessfully to look enthusiastic. It seemed so silly to think that his name should pre-dispose him to an interest in astronomy. He liked the stars just the way Agnes thought of them, as angels' torches. And as in the past, he had the feeling that his future was somehow being decided for him: it might be customary but he didn't like it any the more for that. He didn't *want* to be a scholar – not in the serious way in which the term was used in this family. He'd like to be able to read more Latin poetry, of course, if only to set some of it to music; but the Bible was so rich in stories with vivid enough meaning of their own, that he couldn't understand why everyone seemed to think they needed incessant explanation and comment. In that sense he understood instinctively what Abelard meant about taking nourishment from the fruit of trees, not the leaves. Well, he'd given him something to remember, anyway. *Fructu, non foliis. pomorum quisque cibatur.* The words had a nice cadence.

But all he could think of to say now was: "Yes – and with astronomy I could study music, couldn't I?"

"In the quadrivium. Ye–es. Raoul and Porcarius have told me about your love of music."

"He's very good at it," contributed Charles. "If he hears a tune just once he seems to be able to reproduce it on Grandfather's harp. None of us can do that."

When Louis isn't making fun of me, I can, thought Peter.

"But when I talk of studying music, no one encourages me." Peter risked airing this grudge with a shy sideways look at his father.

"I don't think anyone in our family would discourage you from studying music. But what you perhaps haven't understood is that there's an important distinction between the science of music and the performing of it. Boethius, for example, said that those who devote themselves to playing instruments are cut off from understanding the science of music, since they apply no reason to it, and they don't speculate or make judgements."

If Abelard's apparently gimlet gaze had penetrated his son's heart at that moment he would have gone no further. But, recognizing only the claims of reason and argument, he continued:

"He taught that understanding the science of music is as superior to the act of performance as the mind is superior to the body. The body lives in servitude, devoid of reason . . ."

Peter felt his precarious, treasured talent being trampled by a force he was powerless to resist. So Abelard was, as he had feared he would be, disappointed in him. Well, so be it! He didn't want to be a scholar anyway. Charles could follow the family tradition if he so badly wanted to. He remembered Raoul once saying to

97

Denise and Hugh: "So much variety in one family. In those three older boys you have the makings of a scholar, a knight and a dreamy harper-poet."

But Denise had said sadly, "No, Raoul. 'Harper-poet' puts me in mind of poor Tristan and Isolde. This family has seen enough of tragic love, I think. We want no more legends born here."

Close by the little rubble-stone and timber church they passed the smithy and home of Robert, the blacksmith. As it happened, Raoul's servant had taken the piebald mare to be shod and Fulk was busy at the anvil, under the watchful eye of his father, who leant back against the doorframe. When he caught sight of the three riders approaching their plot of land, Fulk raised the hammer in friendly greeting.

"Fulk – watch what you're doing, you fool," roared Robert, startling the mare, who backed into the servant holding the horse's near hind leg, knocking him off-balance. "You'll *never* make a farrier, let alone a swordwright." But his anger was quickly over, and he sauntered to the gate then to offer his hand to Abelard – in no hurry, for Robert didn't need to rush for anyone, not even for the lord of the manor and his family.

"It's a long time, Master Abelard."

"It is indeed, Robert. God's greetings to you. I see your family has grown up."

"Yes, they're more trouble than ever. It'll soon be time to marry them off, thank the Lord," grinned Robert, pride in his huge offspring written all over his red face.

Peter looked over at Fulk, who had resumed his task, and who made no response to this threat – oh sweet threat, thought Peter – of approaching marriage.

Some little way further on, when the main part of the village lay behind them, they came to a fork in the track, with one branch leading off up into the burnished woodland.

"Ah, that's where we used to go hawking," said Abelard wistfully.

"We could go – later today. Or tomorrow maybe," suggested Charles eagerly.

"I would have liked that, Charles. But I fear that these days my hands are too shaky for a hawk – it'd be confusing for it. It's a strange new affliction with which God has chosen to punish me. But," and he looked nostalgically up the path through the trees, "this was a good spot, especially for partridge and pheasant, as I remember. The forest isn't too dense here."

They rode on in silence for a while, the creak of their saddles and the thud and squelch of hooves suddenly very loud. You could almost taste the sharp freshness of the air after yesterday's rain. A young mother pushed two children past in a long low wheelbarrow, its huge front wheel gouging a rut in the waterlogged track. The little boys waved and stuck their tongues out in excitement, oblivious to rank and fame.

Charles stole a glance at his cousin and understood the glum, closed-in expression on his delicate face. It was Charles – and not Abelard, or Peter – who realized that music might be the one bridge which could unite these two strangers, who were next of kin. Surprised that so sharp a mind as Abelard's had not understood this, he ventured, for his cousin's sake, "But Uncle, to return to the subject of music. It's said that you yourself are an accomplished *performer*. And that you write songs."

"Yes indeed, Charles. I'm sure you know that at one time in my life I wrote a good many secular lyrics which were sung throughout France. But, to go back to what I was saying earlier, Astralabe" – he turned to his son, determined that he should not escape the point – "such activity should be no more than a recreation, a diversion from more serious work based on the Holy Scriptures." Charles was beginning to give up hope – Peter looked so wan, so crushed.

"And recently I've been working on hymn melodies – for the Paraclete." He didn't say that Heloise, now abbess of the Paraclete, had requested them – but both Charles and Peter knew that the Paraclete meant Heloise. "And – something very different – I've written two laments. I have in mind to complete a series of six."

As they turned past the large triangle of Lammas land, which in the early summer months was watched over by Therese's husband, Bernard the hayward, to ensure that the grass would not be stolen before it grew long enough for hay, they had to their right a clear view across the strip-fields. In the distance Hugh was driving the ox-team but in the nearer field the autumn sowing was in full swing. Several of the villagers walked up and down scattering barley seed from the bags slung round their necks, pursued by dozens of children waving their arms in the air and, with cries and laughter, trying without much success to scare away the birds.

Abelard shook his head. "We used to love to do that as children. Until Dagobert actually hit a bird with his hand, and it fell dead on the strip. We knew then it was an omen, and it took away the joy." Dagobert, who came between Abelard and Porcarius, had been the only one of Berengar's sons to take to the military life. A quick-tempered, impetuous, fearless young man – Louis had inherited some of his characteristics together with Abelard's looks – he had been killed at the great battle of Tinchebrai while still in his early twenties.

They were heading now for Little Bend in the Sanguèze, for the vineyards across on the south-facing slopes, and for the mill where old Baudri had met his death.

"Laments?" prompted Charles.

"Yes, I'm attempting to do something new with an old tradition. My laments aren't composed for departed souls, you see, or for actual occasions. Instead, they're based on biblical texts. There are so many themes in the Old Testament which can still quicken our grief, now in the twelfth century of our Lord. I hope to give them new life with tense new rhythms."

"Which themes have you chosen?"

Peter was listening avidly now, grateful for Charles's questions. His own tongue was as if paralyzed. What, he wondered helplessly, had happened to his angry resolve to confront his father about all those things in the past which had left him hurt and bewildered? Above all, his insistence that his mother Heloise should enter a convent. Why was Abelard, in person, somehow more remote than he had been in his imagination? How had his physical presence managed to transform yesterday's burning need to know into what now seemed no more than impertinent curiosity? As they rode, side by side, along bridleways familiar to them both from earliest childhood, it seemed to Peter that the breadth of France had never separated them more effectively.

"Themes such as murder and loss and treachery. The grief of David when he loses his beloved friend Jonathan; of Dinah, daughter of Jacob, whose betrothed is murdered by her own brothers; the pain of Jacob the father when he bids farewell to his young son, Benjamin . . ."

Whether, by working into music another father's ancient grief, Abelard was making some sort of confession, some small offering, Peter would never know. He was aware of a quickening heart-beat, but could only look straight ahead, concentrating on Peggy's twitching ears. So if, in the little silence that followed, father looked at son, the look was not returned. For the son didn't know how, and the father, this of all fathers, had left it too late to teach him.

# 10

When they got back to the manor-house, Abelard went into the Hall to join his brothers and sister, and Peter made his way purposefully down to the kitchens, where he was greeted by the aroma of newly-baked bread. Little Philippe, attracted by the smell, squatted in the corner of the hearth, and gazed longingly at the pile of curvy loaves keeping warm in the ashes. A stew of some sort steamed in its iron pot suspended on a chain above the flames. On a stool in front of the fire, plump legs outstretched, sat Berthe's husband, Girard, as rotund as she was spikily lean. Berthe was of the opinion that she was the only person at Le Pallet who did any work, and it was an opinion she frequently shared with anyone who happened to be within hearing. She was sharing it now, and Peter thought, as he quickly appraised the situation, that Philippe gave Girard a glance of sympathy. Perhaps he was imagining it. But he certainly didn't imagine the slow grin that broke across the child's face when he caught sight of Peter. He got up immediately and led him by the hand to the passageway, where Blanche had made a temporary home in the rushes for her puppies. Three of them were cosily snuggled into the bitch's belly, but the fourth – the only one to have dark-coloured markings in its pale grey fur – lay a little apart. Despite himself, Peter experienced a pang of pity for the minute, helpless creature. "It's *only* a dog," he reminded himself, as Agatha had pointed out. It was said that animals didn't have feelings, but anyone who'd ridden Peggy more than a few times knew better.

"Yes, you'd better get rid of that runt, Master Peter. She don't get a look-in at the teats."

"All right, I will. That's why I'm here. But you didn't have to tease Agnes like that, Berthe," reproached Peter.

"What a *fuss*! It's only a dog. There are too many of them around this place as it is."

"Maybe. But Agnes is only a child. She doesn't understand," and Peter stooped to pick up the tiny animal, much to Philippe's excitement.

"And *you* nearly a man. You should have better things to concern yourself with. A fine knight you'll make," snorted Berthe. Peter knew that it was only half a jest, and there *was* a little part of him that felt ashamed. But he said firmly: "I'll concern myself with what I think fit." He saw through the kitchen arch that Girard was winking approval at him. Berthe was a conscientious, loyal servant but her grumpiness, unlike old Thomas's in the stables, often had a sharp edge of spite to it, and Peter was in no mood for that today. Some junkets were cooling in earthenware dishes and, as he passed, he dipped a finger in each one in turn, simply to annoy her.

"Just seeing if they'd set," he called jauntily back across his shoulder as he left the kitchen with the puppy, and with Philippe – who had exactly imitated his new hero's treatment of the junkets – close on his heels.

Outside he let Philippe stroke the miniature dog before tucking it inside his shirt and tunic and fetching Peggy from her tethering at the well. Philippe followed, whimpering.

"No, Philippe, not today. Go back inside now." No one knew how much the boy understood in words, but the firmness in Peter's tone was clear and the whimpering stopped. Philippe just stood there, looking forlornly after rider and pony as they disappeared out of the courtyard.

Berthe was right, reflected Peter, as he rode back towards Maud's shack – for that's what he had decided to do. He'd had the idea when they stopped earlier with Abelard to exchange a few words with her. He ought to be concerning himself with other things. Well, he wasn't going to be a knight any more than a scholar. He'd leave that to Louis. Though what he was going to be was rather less certain – and for the moment he didn't really care. His life was dominated now by only two figures. Just two. (Not even the puppy was a diversion, for what he was doing confessedly for Agnes he was doing, obliquely, for her nursemaid, Nicolette.) Or was there, always waiting in the shadows of his mind, a third? Was there not room for Heloise beside Nicolette and Abelard?

Maud was sitting beside her own little fire, holding her shoes out over it to dry them. A pot, of clay not iron, sat in the embers and an unskinned rabbit hung from a pole above. She started when Peter called her name, for she was becoming quite deaf and had not heard him approach.

Peter produced the tiny puppy, which was so weak that it scarcely moved in his hand.

"Maud, can you do anything with this? Agnes wanted it so badly for her own, but it's the runt and will certainly die in a day or so. I was going to get rid of it, but then I thought what a wonderful surprise Agnes would have if . . ."

The old woman had been making cheese earlier, and Peter caught the smell of sour milk which surrounded her. She shook her head up at him. "You are too soft for your own good, Master Peter. But yes, give me the

105

puppy. We'll see what can be done for Miss Agnes."

"Maud, you're always there when you're needed," said Peter gratefully. The little tribute brought a blush to her face, which, Peter thought sadly, was beginning to look very lined.

"So you've seen your father," she stated simply.

"Yes." She saw the closed-in expression, heard the defensive tone.

"He was greatly changed since last I saw him. But, after all, that *was* just after you were born."

"Do you mean he looks old? I think he seems strong and energetic still, though I believe his neck still troubles him from a fall he had from his horse." For some reason Peter didn't want to think of his father as old.

"No, he's not old. Not yet. And yes, he still rides straight and proud, and his gaze is dark and unblinking as ever it was. Those are the things he's remembered for in the village. Nay, t'was something else that struck me, Master Peter. Your father has a mistrust in his face, a loneliness."

Peter explained, "I believe that for many years now he's gone in fear of his life. At St Gildas, the monks were barbarians, so my Aunt Denise has said. It's Brittany still, but it could be another world up there – I believe he's suffered a great deal."

"And I don't think his sufferings are over. Part kindly from him, Master Peter – you may not meet again."

Peter looked sharply at the old woman, who, they said, could see into the future. What was she telling him?

"What do you mean, Maud? Is he going to die?"

"Of course. Though not yet, I don't think. But I sense he has more battles, big battles, to fight. And he's a lonely man."

Peter remembered how distant, how remote his

father had seemed even as he talked to him, riding side by side. He knew that Maud was right. But what could *he* do about it? Why did Abelard deserve all the pity? Was he, Peter, not lonely too, his bad, abandoned child? Son of the eunuch and his now holy whore. He dismounted from Peggy and, uninvited, sat down on the rough bench beside Maud's hut. She sat beside him. Peggy wandered away to the grass under the pear tree, frightening away Maud's two sheep.

She went on, "I'm not a clever woman, and you know very well that I have no learning. But I see a lot of things from my little corner of this valley. And what I see, I know. You say your father has suffered. Well, I've lived a long time and I've seen two sorts of suffering – or two things which suffering can do. The one opens our ears to the songs of sadness in other hearts; the second hears only the laments within."

Peter gouged a dent in the damp earth with his shoe.

"And Abelard?"

"As I said, he seems a lonely man." Maud's answer was a little enigmatic, but Peter thought he knew what she meant.

He puzzled over it for a while and then said, "But he's accepted his suffering. Uncle Porcarius says that Abelard quickly came to accept what happened as a just punishment from God. His devotion to God is beyond question, Maud – you seem to be saying that he complains." As he talked, Peter grew flushed; to his own amazement he began to rise to his father's defence. But how uncomfortably strange it was that she had used the word 'laments'.

"I never questioned his devotion to God, Master Peter – or his acceptance of suffering. I just see what I see, and hear – deaf though I am – what I hear." As she talked, she dipped a dirty-nailed finger into a pail of milk standing beside her, and let the puppy, lying inert in her lap, sniff and then gradually begin to lick it.

Peter wanted to get up and leave, but he also wanted to stay. Despite, or perhaps because of her eccentricities, there was something calm and understanding about Maud.

"I'm still not sure I understand what you mean. About the two sorts of suffering."

"You will, Master Peter, you will. And for now, do you see what has just happened?"

"No." He looked around, misunderstanding her.

"You're looking in the wrong direction. It's inside you should look. This morning, when you all passed by and stopped to talk, I saw the look on your face, and I saw the way you rode off – all stiff and sulky. There was a song of sadness in *your* heart, if I'm not very mistaken. But now look at you! All dark eyes in defence of the stranger who is your father. Doesn't that tell you something?"

Yes, it told him a great deal; or rather, it gave new force to something he'd dimly known all his remembered life. It told him that deep beneath all the layers of disappointment and doubt there still existed between him and his parent – if not the other way round – a primitive and powerful bond which had nothing to do with love. Maud had understood that. Maud, solitary but not lonely on the edge of other people's lives, had *seen* that.

For the second time in two weeks Peter left her shack in reflective mood. For a change he took the slightly longer way home around the orchards instead of along the river track. Drawing near to the sheds where the cattle were housed in the winter, he saw that he wasn't the only one to have chosen that path. Head bowed in thought, one hand clasping her dark cloak below her chin, Nicolette was a hundred yards or so ahead of him.

In a moment Abelard and his sufferings were forgotten; Peter urged the pony forward and quickly caught up with her.

She turned at the sound of the hoofbeats, and smiled up at him the sweet dancing smile which had first so bewitched him on Michaelmas night.

"What brings you here?" he asked.

"Oh – I've been to see my sister Constance. To tell her to come up to the manor-house to sew Grandfather's shroud with me. Lady Denise is going to help us." There was no resentment in her tone, but it occurred to Peter that it should not have been up to Nicolette to make this arrangement with her elder sister. He dismounted and walked along beside her, leading Peggy by the reins. He wasn't sure whether to admit what *he* had been doing.

Then, deciding that she would be pleased for Agnes's sake, he confided, "I've been to see Maud. She's going to try and raise that puppy for Agnes." Nicolette chuckled with pleasure. He saw how the little arrow-head birthmark above her left brow contracted when she laughed and he wanted more than ever to kiss it.

"Master Peter, you're so good to those girls." Then, more shyly, "You're their favourite, you know."

"I know." And Peter grinned at her, for once, briefly, pleased with himself. It didn't seem to matter to her that what he had done might be less than manly, less than worthy of the concerns of a knight. The larks, who had been singing all day, burst into song in the high blue-washed vaults of the October sky.

Exultant, he said: "You don't have to call me 'Master Peter' all the time, you know."

"But it's right that I should. And after all I could never address Master Charles as Charles – or Master Louis as Louis."

Did a small cloud pass across the sun? Did at that moment the larks fall quiet? Or did it just seem so?

"Do you *have* to address us all in the same way?"

"It's right that I should," Nicolette repeated firmly, certain of her place.

"Then you must do as seems right to you. But, Nicolette, all morning I've been worried about that terrible thing I said to you outside the stables."

"I think that on a ride with your father you should have had more important things on your mind."

"No, indeed, I did not. And I would not have hurt you, if the Kingdom of Heaven had been my reward."

There, he had said it now. Given himself away. Gone beyond the point of no return.

She was silent for a while as she skipped over a puddle in the track. Then, ignoring the weight in his words, she said, "You didn't hurt me. Such things are easily said." But she was too shy to look at him, and he at her.

They went on in silence. Over to their right the sowing was still going on in the fields, a penumbra of crows and starlings following its slow progress. Then Nicolette, who was not easy with silence, said in her artless way, "It's such a beautiful day – but I'm ashamed to be glad at this time." Peter received the little confidence as a gift. Gently, he replied: "I don't think it's wrong to feel glad. Baudri was an old man and he is with Christ, I'm sure. And after all, the sunshine, too, is a gift from God."

They were now approaching the main pathway which bisected the orchards and led up to the house. As they turned the corner Peter pointed ahead to 'his' apple tree with a dismissive laugh, "I used to sit in that tree when I was a child. That was where I went to sulk when I had a quarrel with – with anyone, or when I was in trouble." Why did he have this need to share

110

things with her, as if her very knowing blessed them, made them more precious?

But she, perhaps relieved that the conversation seemed to have taken a less intense turn, confessed, "I had a place like that, too. In the loft over the dairy. Until one day Constance found out and took the ladder away and I was stuck up there until dark. Mother was *furious*!"

They both laughed. But as they passed by his tree he gave it a valedictory glance. "When I was a child," he had said, with less than total honesty, to Nicolette – but he knew that he'd never again be able to retreat to its familiar branches for safety and comfort. For children, he told himself firmly, do not fall in love.

Meanwhile Abelard and Denise had withdrawn to the solar for some privacy. Hugh was still out on the estate attending to the ploughing and the sowing with Charles and Louis. Porcarius was asleep in the Hall, and Raoul, accompanied by Ralph, had taken his piebald mare back to Robert as one of the shoes which Fulk had fitted seemed to be loose. The little girls, who had just learned how to spin, were practising in the corner of the solar.

"You have some documents you want me to put in safekeeping for you, brother?"

"Yes. I've written an account of my misfortunes and there is some correspondence – four letters to date – which Heloise, my dear sister in Christ, and I have written to each other. There are copies with her at the abbey of the Paraclete, but life is so full of vicissitudes and my enemies are so numerous that I was anxious for another copy to be preserved. Poor Thibault – it was one of his last labours for me before those butchers killed him instead of me. He even made the ink for the copies – from hawthorn bushes near St Gildas."

"Peter used to call hawthorn berries 'bloodberries' when he was little," offered Denise. But Abelard was deep in his thoughts, and didn't reply.

She laid her hand on his shoulder as she passed him to go and sort out a knot in Agatha's spinning. The gesture seemed to remind him of the pain in his neck, for he put his left hand to it and moved it lightly up and down.

"There's also a long letter in verse which I have composed for Peter. Just general words of advice which he would do well to heed now that he's almost a man . . . Do you think he is fitted more for scholarship or the life of a knight?"

"I don't know," she answered thoughtfully, as she threaded a large needle. "He doesn't have the great intellect of either of his parents" – and she gave him a swift glance – "though his mind is quick enough and he has a strong will. But his real talent is in music – and that I think he has from you, brother."

"Yes, we've talked about that – it is a useful enough gift to have. But I find him a quiet boy. And he is so uncannily like Heloise when I first desired her that – I cannot explain this to you."

Denise looked up in surprise. It was unlike Abelard to be bereft of words. Seeing how she expected him to go on, he said, "That song is sung, Denise. Read the letters and you will understand that that song, that wantonly impure song, is sung." He sounded impatient, almost angry, though at what she couldn't at first be sure. Then she thought she understood and nearly said, 'And it's hard when you come face to face with the living echo?' But she stopped herself in time, for suddenly the connection between an impure song, Abelard's way of describing his love affair with Heloise, and its necessarily tainted echo – its offspring – was monstrously clear to her.

112

Peter's own words came back to her now, charged with new meaning.

"Was it bad luck when I was born? A bad child – leading to Abelard's punishment from God?" No, she shouldn't have dismissed the question as she had – it had cried out for more careful attention. Abelard, meanwhile, had for once turned his direct gaze away, and was staring into the fire.

She paused for several long moments. She knew that she risked hurting her brother, but she also knew that she might never have another chance to talk to him about Peter. Slowly she said, "I think he is like Heloise in more than appearance. He's a passionate, vulnerable child. Sometimes I fear for him because he feels things so deeply."

"What sort of things?"

She reflected for a moment. No, she couldn't spare him this: Abelard should know.

"He broods about the past. He doesn't understand what happened and he is hurt by not understanding."

Abelard was watching her needle. "But why should he be hurt?" he asked, puzzled.

She looked up again, abruptly, startled. With some vehemence she repeated, "*Why?*"

"Yes, why? After all, it's hardly as if he was abandoned. We entrusted him to the care of a good family – *my* family – in the place of my own childhood, where we knew he would be cared for and loved and taught to honour God." Abelard seemed genuinely bewildered.

"And he has indeed been loved. I've loved him as my own child; no, there are times when I think he is dearer to me even than my own children. Perhaps because of the way he came to be mine. Abelard, it's because I cherish him that I have such anxiety for him."

"What pain can there be for a child not yet sixteen,

who has had every advantage which life can offer, raised in the knowledge of Jesus Christ, surrounded by kith and kin, and every physical comfort . . ?" There was now a hard edge to his voice, but Denise was no longer afraid of speaking her mind. She lay down her tapestry, unable to concentrate on it, and paced up and down. Agnes, sensing her mother's tension, ran to her and clung to her skirt, looking at her unfamiliar uncle with huge suspicious eyes.

Denise's own eyes were equally large and accusing now with the pent-up and unacknowledged anger of fifteen long years. All she had wanted was for Abelard to talk to Peter, to help him understand why they had left him, so uncompromisingly, behind. But that Abelard himself could be so uncomprehending – so blind, so deaf – was a devastating shock to her.

"You say you didn't abandon him. But how do you think it seems to him, to have a father who deigns to visit him twice in nearly sixteen years; who has written him not one word of comfort, whose mother turned her back on him as an infant of not much more than three months, still suckling? In my understanding, my *mother's* understanding, *that* – Abelard – is abandonment."

"Denise, control yourself." Abelard, too, had risen, his eyes glittering almost black in a face drawn taut and pale. But he spoke with measured calm.

"I had no idea – at the time it seemed right – I had no idea you would be a reluctant foster-mother. But it was a burden for you, it *is* true – Louis had scarcely stopped suckling himself."

Denise was now almost beside herself. "How *dare* you suggest my anger is because I had no room in my heart for the child. I have told you; he is as dear to me as any of my own. What I resent is the way you simply rode out of his life – as if he meant nothing more to

114

you." Agnes started to cry and Agatha now came and hung on the other side of her mother's skirt. Denise put a hand to her face, and pushed away her stray lock of hair. She could scarcely believe she had spoken in such a way to Abelard, her revered brother, her adored brother, her suffering brother, to whom her loyalty had always been – outwardly – so complete.

She sat down again, heavily. Immediately the memory of Abelard's own troubles began to flood in on her. For years he had gone in fear of his life; he had been forced to burn, with his own hands, his great book on the Trinity, fruit of years of work; he had suffered outrage to his body – and he had lost the only woman he had ever loved. Oh, perhaps she had had no right to speak out so.

"I feel as if there were an arrow in my heart," she said softly.

"There is no need for such talk. I'm glad you are calmer. Truly, sister, I believe you fear unnecessarily for Peter. I only pray to God that he never experiences real anguish – the like of which I have had to suffer. When you read my account you will know the meaning of pain." His tone was again bewildered, and a little hurt, a little self-righteous.

"I know how you've suffered, Abelard – in every part of your life. And God in heaven knows that we who love you have despaired at being powerless to help you. The last thing I wanted was to cause you more distress. But I suddenly felt so angry, perhaps because I've so often seen the sadness in his eyes."

"It will be the sadness of a young man about to leave his childhood behind. But as to your reproach that I have not communicated with him; I assure you, sister, that it was not through indifference, but because I had such confidence in you and your good husband Hugh. It didn't occur to me that you – or Peter – might have need of me."

It was an honest reason. Abelard never lied and to make false excuses was against both his nature and the high moral standards which he now always set himself. But, despite being flattered at the implicit compliment, its very honesty gave Denise bleak new insight into the brother she thought she had known.

Yet her anger was spent now. She told the girls to get on with their spinning and said to Abelard, "Let me show you where we keep the special documents. We have a safe place in the wall behind the tapestry there."

"Have you no wish to see them first?" Abelard sounded surprised.

"I assumed they would be private."

"I have nothing to hide from my family. Nor, I think, does Heloise – even when she was my mistress my songs to her were sung all over France, as she herself makes mention in one of her letters. Now that she is no longer dear to me in the world, but dear to me as a sister in Christ – as you, Denise, are my sister in the flesh – what could there be to conceal? No, I think it's right that my family, who love us, should understand the pain that has been ours."

At this mention of Heloise, Denise looked at him curiously.

"And Peter?"

"Especially Peter."

"There is nothing in there that would hurt him more?"

"He will, I am sure, feel hurt on our behalf. His would be a cold heart if he didn't."

"But is there perhaps a little particular comfort for him, too?"

"Perhaps. Especially if he follows the advice I offer him in my long letter in verse – and that will not be easy as he goes through life."

116

"I thought perhaps something personal . . ." Denise wasn't quite sure what she was expecting, but she assumed that any letters between Abelard and Heloise must contain references to Peter, and that these could bring him either more distress or understanding and solace.

"I'm not sure I understand what you ask. But you should read the documents, sister, and make your own judgements."

Denise grimaced.

"Oh, Denise – your *Latin*?"

She blushed. "I know, Abelard. All your efforts when you came home ill from Paris and stayed for those six years – but I was a young girl then, I can't have been more than sixteen when you left again – and that's a very long time ago. And I never was a very good student, was I?"

"You didn't concentrate, that was your trouble. You weren't without ability, but you had all the distractions of a young woman growing up on a country estate."

"Yes, I preferred riding and hawking and helping in the dairy. It all seemed much more important than learning about the ancients."

"And Raoul and Porcarius? Haven't they given you a little encouragement from time to time?"

"They used to, after you first left. What with your brilliance, Porcarius's humour and Raoul's gentle patience I should have been – well, perhaps half as clever as Heloise. Porcarius used to say that as teachers you were the only trinity that amounted to less than one whole, because I made so little progress!"

"Porcarius's humour, then as now, comes dangerously close to blasphemy at times. But Heloise, you must remember, was exceptional in her gift for scholarship. She was famous for it even before I became her

117

teacher. Learning is not the work of most women."

"Indeed not. And once I was married – well, you know how busy our mother Lucie always was. It was the same for me. But I would dearly love to read your account, brother – and with the help of . . ." She was interrupted by Agatha running past her to open the oak door to the stairway, having heard a quiet knock. It was Nicolette.

"I'm sorry to disturb you, my lady, but you said to see you when I got back – about the shroud."

"Of course, Nicolette. Come in, come in."

Abelard rose, taking his cue.

"I will leave you women to your task. It's nearly time to say vespers in any case." And with a polite bow he left the room, stooping as he passed through the low doorway.

## 11

Two days later, early on Saturday evening, they buried
Baudri. The time was chosen specially so that
Abelard's hymn 'Vespers: Saturday evening', which
Raoul had heard once before and recognized as mag-
nificent, could be sung at the service.

"I scarcely think our little village church is the place
for such a work. None of the peasants will sing properly
and it'll be spoilt," Hugh had protested, anxious not to
mar in any way what he wanted, quite properly, to be
a truly village affair. There was no question of using
the family chapel which was far too tiny.

Denise and her brothers felt differently and Raoul
had taken him aside and persuaded him. "There are
enough of us to do it some justice and there'll be a
psalm and another hymn for the villagers. Baudri
would have been honoured by such a farewell, Hugh."

The funeral was indeed a village affair. As soon as
the priest began tolling the bell in its squat rubble-
stone tower, a group began to cluster and swell around
the entrance to the little timber-roofed church. The
coffin was transported on a mule cart to the edge of the
village, where the procession of chief mourners gathered
to lift and bear it on its slow way along the central
bridleway. As it approached, Robert and his eldest
sons Fulk and Guy began to ring their handbells to
ward off evil spirits, while others – the thick-set miller
married to Constance and Raymond the falconer
among them – beat a dirge on their tabors. Abelard led

the mourners, holding only his breviary, followed by Porcarius and Raoul, each with lighted tapers. Hugh, Charles, Louis and Peter – for Baudri had no surviving male relatives of his own – bore the coffin, a black cloth, embroidered with a gold cross by Nicolette and Constance, with Denise's help, draped over its convex lid. Everyone who could crowded through the rounded zigzag-carved archway after the procession, whose members took their seats on the rough wooden benches. Peter, turning to look for a place after depositing the sad burden onto the chancel flagstones, saw there was one on the end of the front bench next to Nicolette. He was just about to take it when Louis stepped neatly sideways from the back corner of the coffin and got there first. Peter had no choice but to slip onto the next bench, where he found himself standing behind Agatha and Agnes and their mother, with Nicolette – whom Denise was treating as family – and Louis on the right in front of him.

There wasn't room for everyone in the church, which consisted of just a simple chancel and nave with narrow aisle, so there was much muttering and shuffling of feet as everyone struggled to get a view. The priest, a very pale, blonde young man from Nantes, who had recently taken up his position as cleric to the three neighbouring manors, was rather overawed by today's illustrious company. When he eventually stopped tolling the bell, a reverent quiet descended. A moment or two later Abelard's high, resonant voice rang out to start the only service he would ever conduct in the parish of his birth.

Peter at first tried hard to concentrate, as his father uttered prayers for the dead man ". . . that the soul of this your servant may be brought by the hands of your holy angels . . ." but he simply could not wrench his eyes and his thoughts away from the figure in front of him ". . . to the bosom of your friend the patriarch Abraham . . ." and the metal ring which held her headdress in place glinted in the light of Raoul's taper in the aisle, mocking him from close below Louis's high broad shoulder ". . . may be raised again on the last day of the great judgement . . ." and, as Louis looked down at his small neighbour, presumably with a smile of condolence, Peter's heart swelled with murderous intent.

Never before had he failed to close his eyes during prayer (even if the mind behind the eyes had wandered from time to time in the past), never before had he felt sick at the smell of incense, never before had any of the words of the Athanasian creed eluded him. Ashamed, he prayed for forgiveness, prayed for mercy and thus forgot in self-absorption to pray for Baudri's soul. The only thing he did right was to follow the command to pray for strength for the bereaved. And, when they came at the end to offer up Abelard's great hymn, *Quanta qualia sunt*, in which he had likened life in heaven to an endless succession of glorious, peaceful sabbaths, the words of blissful devotion had for Peter a new and wholly worldly sense: *si quantum sentiunt possint exprimere*, 'if any word can utter the fullness of the heart'. Never had *his* heart been so corrupt, as in God's own house it overflowed with love and hate; indeed it was as if his whole body were too frail to contain the turmoil within.

In the few days that Abelard spent at Le Pallet before and after the funeral, he helped Charles and Peter – and Louis, when he couldn't think of a pressing enough excuse to escape – with their studies. If those hours didn't succeed in bringing Peter any closer to his father, they did at least increase his appreciation of the clarity of thought, the sheer force and boldness of intellect which hundreds of students had found – and would again find – so magnetic. It wasn't so much that Abelard persuaded; there was in his arguments something more elemental than persuasion. He would repeat and present the views of people he disagreed with so that they sounded perfectly reasonable, and then he would, with the power of wind or water, simply obliterate them.

It so happened that before leaving St Gildas he had started on a philosophical work which he planned to publish under the title 'Know thyself', and which had particular relevance to Peter's state of mind at that time. Perhaps from a wish to talk about ideas which were not yet fully formulated, perhaps in response to Charles's eager questions, Abelard talked to them about it at some length.

His chief argument in the work was that good and evil do not lie in our deeds, but in our intentions – that it is the attitudes of a man rather than the nature of his actions that God judges. "If we do wrong," he told them, "believing it to be right, God would not consider us guilty." Charles looked startled and Louis rather less bored when Abelard then gave as an illustration: "The divine law, for example, forbids us to sleep with our sisters, but if in later life you were to meet and lie with a woman who, unbeknown to you, happened to be your sister, then you couldn't be blamed for the act because you performed it in ignorance. It is a similar thing with charity. I know you boys have seen little of beggars, living as you do on a plentiful country estate, but imagine that you come to Paris and feel pity for some old man, hungry and in rags, who is begging on your street. If you approach him with the intention of giving him alms but are unable to do so, perhaps because you find you have no money after all, you would not then be transgressing against the law that

122

tells you to love your neighbour as yourself. The point is that the good will was there, though the opportunity may have been missing. As I said, God does not judge us by what we do, but by what frame of mind we do it in."

For Peter, the implications of these arguments were terrifying. Only yesterday he had stood in the village church harbouring the most evil thoughts. Had he not actively wished, no – actively *willed* – something to happen to remove Louis so that he, Peter, could woo Nicolette without threat of competition. If sin lay in the will then he, surely, was damned. He was almost relieved when Louis himself challenged:

"So, Uncle, you are saying that if I desire to sleep with a woman who is not my wife, then that desire is in itself a sin?"

Abelard turned his attention to Louis, whose features he couldn't help but recognize as so similar to his own. But he recognized too the hint of irony in his nephew's voice; he was no stranger to mockery as a reaction to his radical ideas and, if he regretted hearing a trace of it now within his own family, he gave no sign.

"No, Louis, I'm not saying that. It's in *consenting* to the desire to sin that we transgress. It is not a sin to lust after another man's wife, but only to consent to that lust. It is the consent alone that is sinful – not the temptation which comes first, nor the doing of the deed which comes after."

"So I can lust after any woman I choose without incurring guilt – as long as I don't give in to my desire?"

Charles and Peter were both becoming distinctly uneasy, but for different reasons. Charles, like most people, believed there were deeds which were evil in themselves and therefore worthy of divine punishment whatever the intentions behind them, and so he was fascinated by his uncle's unorthodox arguments and irritated that Louis kept limiting them to the question of sexual desire. Peter, though slightly relieved by the answer about consent – for, after all, he hadn't actually *consented* to any sinful act as yet – was horribly certain that Louis's talk of lust referred to a specific person.

"No, that's not right either. Remember what our Lord said: 'Whoever shall look on a woman to lust after her, hath already committed adultery in his heart.'"

Louis shrugged, beginning to get bored again. "I don't understand all this." But Abelard was patient. He had earned his reputation as a teacher for far more difficult tasks of explanation than this, and Louis was scarcely a serious challenge.

"It may be easier to look at it like this, Louis. You can be tempted to have intercourse with a woman. That in itself is not a sin; it is, in fact, inevitable in the human condition. But if you say to yourself as you look at her: 'I desire you and at the first opportunity I will lie with you', then in your mind you have consented to the desire, which to begin with was neither good nor evil. You become guilty when you fail to put up a fight against it."

Peter wasn't at all sure where all this left his soul and its chances of salvation, but he was glad when Louis got up.

"Yes, I see. But if you'll excuse me I promised Thomas I'd check on Esprit. He has an infection in a hind hoof. Thank you, Uncle," he added, without conviction, as he whistled to the two hounds in the Hall and took his leave. Louis wasn't sure if he'd been made a fool of and he needed the security of the stable, where he felt totally in control, to restore his self-confidence. In the courtyard he came upon Porcarius, who was ambling up and down, reading.

"Hello, Louis! Had enough philosophy? It's a pity

not to make the most of this opportunity – there are plenty who'd envy you."

"It's not for me, all that. I'll happily leave philosophy to the scholars."

"Ah well! It takes many sorts of men to make up our world. Just because you're so like Abelard physically, it's foolish to expect you to take after him in other ways."

"Not physically like him in every respect, I hope."

"Louis! That was a cheap, unworthy joke at the expense of a kinsman's tragedy. Quite intolerable. I thank God your mother didn't hear it." Porcarius's small blue eyes almost disappeared in his outrage.

The rebuke, coming from the uncle whose own jokes were sometimes near the borders of good taste, was a serious one. A blush suffused Louis's handsome features. He realized that such a remark had not been worthy of a knight, and he was glad his father hadn't heard it.

"I apologize, Uncle. But it's so easy for *him* to moralize about lust and such things – I got impatient with it."

"That's no excuse. I suggest you go straight to the chapel to pray for forgiveness. But we will not speak of it further." He turned abruptly away, unwilling to be drawn into discussion about whether or not it was easy for Abelard to moralize on sexual matters.

Back at the trestle table in the Great Hall, Charles and Peter continued to listen to Abelard with rapt attention. It occurred to Peter, sitting beside his father, that it must have been in just such a situation that his mother first fell in love with him. He tried to look at Abelard through that other pair of eyes. The fine head of grey-white hair around the tonsure, the regular profile with its long straight nose and fine forehead, small well-shaped ears below which curled one little lock of hair – he was, for fifty-five, an extremely good-looking man. But it was only when one looked at him face to face that you felt the full force of his appeal, for it was those bright, near-black eyes which warned of the glare of his mind.

Abelard was further illustrating his point about deeds not being good or evil in themselves. "If, for example, two men hang a convict, the one because of a desire for justice, the other out of hatred arising from an old enmity, then – although they both perform the same act and both do what justice requires because the man they hang is a criminal – the one does well, the other sins. Do you understand?"

"So-o," said Charles slowly, earnestly struggling with the implications of what was being said, "does that mean that however bad an act may seem, it's not a sin if it's done in ignorance, or good faith? I mean – I'm trying to think of the worst thing I can – well, take those who crucified our Lord."

"You'll be a good student, Charles." Abelard touched his nephew's shoulder in a rare gesture of approval. "Yes, that's exactly what I'm saying. 'Father, forgive them, for they know not what they do.' "

Charles drew in his breath sharply, half-appalled, half-seduced by the temerity of this argument. Even Peter, momentarily jolted out of his mood of brooding introspection, looked sideways at his father with a new interest. There were so many things he would have liked to ask – about how to tell the difference between vice and virtue, about repentance and forgiveness – but Charles had made such an obviously intelligent comment and received such approval that Peter was afraid of seeming stupid in comparison. Worse still, his questions might betray just how bad a person he really was. He also had the disadvantage of not knowing

126

how he should address the teacher; 'father' would have seemed false and contrived; 'Master Abelard' was out of the question. No one had given him any guidance on this rather subtle point and his uncertainty about it became in itself a sort of barrier. At that moment, however, there was a small diversion.

The door opened to reveal Berthe carrying a wooden tray with platters, beakers and a bowl of fruit. Marie, one of the village girls who helped Berthe in the kitchen, continued to stand against the door, holding it open for Agnes and Agatha, who had been downstairs meddling with the puppies and then been pressed into service. Agnes proudly carried a loaf of bread under each arm and Agatha, with a frown of exaggerated concentration, walked in gingerly with a pitcher full of milk. Before they reached the long oak dining table, some distance away from Abelard and the boys, one of the dogs, who had followed them and who was almost as big as Agatha, sidled up to her to sniff what she was carrying. It jogged her arm and, startled, Agatha succeeded in spilling half the contents of the pitcher, which of course brought forth a string of reproaches from Berthe. Agatha began to cry, while the dogs nosed around in the now warm and soggy rushes.

"That's enough, Berthe – she didn't mean to spill it," called out Charles, irritated at having this most fascinating of lessons interrupted by mere meal preparations.

"Exactly – not very sinful," said Abelard himself, smiling benevolently at his tearful niece. And to the boys: "A nice little domestic illustration of what we've just been discussing!"

Peter was watching the open door, expecting Nicolette to be near at hand. Abelard was just gathering up his manuscripts when she did appear, rather out of breath and flustered, and Peter couldn't help noticing that neither his father nor Charles scarcely even glanced at her. How *could* they be so indifferent? She dropped a shy curtsey in their direction and then called to the girls to come and prepare themselves for the meal. Peter was almost suffocated by a swell of love as he watched the slight figure disappear up the stairway at the north end of the Hall. It gave to his earlier unspoken questions about good and evil a new urgency, for now he needed reassurance that this glorious new dimension which life had so suddenly revealed was not in itself sinful. He no longer cared if it sounded stupid.

So he blurted out, "Is it always possible to tell when a desire or a feeling is good or bad? I mean – is it always wrong to consent to the wish to eat good food, or – to, well, love a woman?"

Peter Abelard looked keenly at his young son at that moment.

"I'm glad you asked that, Astralabe! There are indeed those who would say that fleshly pleasure always increases sin. To them I would put the question: 'Why would the Lord, the creator of foods, put such flavours into them if it would be impossible for us to eat them without sin?' But in judging whether your intentions are good or evil, my son, and therefore whether you can give in to them, look inwards, know yourself – *scito te ipsum* – and decide whether they are governed by love or by greed. For, as the blessed Augustine said, every one of Christ's commands concerned only those two things – love and greed."

Peter nodded sagely, as if he understood. And, in fact, he did understand – or he did with his mind. It was, after all, an easy clear-cut distinction; love was something you gave to others, greed or lust prompted you to take for yourself. Yet, as he looked over towards the north stairway which had just swallowed Nicolette's figure, he realized that in recent days he had fallen heir to a different sort of understanding that had nothing to do with the workings of the mind. And it was this other winged, unreasoning wisdom, older than the teaching of St Augustine, more ancient still than the commands of Christ, which told him that easy, clear-cut distinctions had no place in that love which a man could feel for a woman: a love in which the urge to give and the urge to take were blended in one great sublime upheaval.

---

## 12

Although Peter felt no less awkward with Abelard at the end of his brief stay at Le Pallet than at the beginning, he did at least start to get used to the awkwardness. Perhaps it even became a little less paralyzing. He would never know whether, in time, it might have melted away altogether. As it was, he awoke on the morning of Abelard's departure – barely a week after his arrival – with a panicky feeling that there were still many questions unanswered. If he didn't ask these things now, there might never be another chance.

It had been decided at short notice that Hugh and Louis would accompany Abelard and his new servant on the first stretch of their journey to Paris, turning northwards at Angers towards an estate on the borders of Brittany and Anjou, where Hugh hoped to place Louis as a squire with some relatives of the Count of Brittany. Porcarius would also be with them as far as Angers, where he worked as an administrator in the cathedral chapter.

Peter and Charles were to ride with the little party as far as the road to Angers but, as all the others wanted to come with them to the ford on Great Bend, they had to start off on foot, leading the horses. They hadn't got much further than the drawbridge before Peter gave in to Agatha's entreaties to be allowed to ride Peggy, while Peter kept her on a short rein. Seeing her sister so favoured, Agnes began to make a fuss and so Louis, with one flowing movement, scooped the little girl from the ground, lifted her above his head and planted her on his shoulders. Nicolette, laughing up into her charge's delighted face, reached out a hand to pat one dangling foot.

"There's a nice ride for you!" she exclaimed. Peter was incensed; he couldn't remember Louis ever paying so much attention to his sister, and he deeply suspected the motive.

In front of them Denise and Abelard were walking together.

"I've said this to Hugh and now I want to say it to you, Denise: we did well to leave our son with you despite the feelings you expressed the other day. With your good guidance he has become a serious-minded and God-fearing young man." Denise knew that this was the nearest she would come to receiving praise or gratitude, and she was torn between pleasure at the compliment and, despite herself, a little rush of resentment. Did all the years of devotion and commitment to her brother's son not warrant just a little more recognition? Was there not, after all, more to Peter than a serious mind and a Christian faith, important though these things were? But for all that she said, "I pray that one day he will be worthy of his two remarkable parents." The respect in her voice was genuine. Denise was only too aware of the solemnity of the occasion; it might be many years before Abelard made the journey back to Le Pallet. If, indeed, he ever would.

They were almost at the ford. Everyone stopped. Abelard placed his hands on Ralph's and then his nieces' heads – both now safely returned to firm ground – to bless them; he embraced his brother Raoul, and then leant down and kissed Denise tenderly on the forehead.

"May God bless and keep you, my sister," he said,

with an earnestness which brought the ready tears brimming to her eyes.

Swallowing hard, she managed, "You too, you too, Abelard."

Peter, watching the workings of her face, was strangely unmoved. He too would have liked to summon tears of farewell, but his source was dry.

When he looked back after coaxing a reluctant Peggy across the ford, Raoul had linked his arm through Denise's as they stood waving, and Ralph, quite unaffected by the occasion, was already chasing the girls back along the path, his arms raised under his cloak in some grotesque parody of a bird of prey. Nicolette, her dark unbraided hair blowing around her shoulders in the keen October wind, stood motionless, looking rather wistfully after the riders.

Peter was about to raise a hand to wave to her but then thought better of it; after all, it wasn't he who was going away.

As they rode along the northern bank of the Sangueze, Abelard dropped back to speak privately to Peter.

"There are two things I want to say to you before we part, my son." Peter's eyes lit up with hope. But still he wasn't sure how to address his father, so he simply bowed courteously and slowed Peggy down to the other horse's pace.

"Firstly, I am troubled by the thought that when you go out into the world you will hear my enemies – who are numerous – cast doubt on my faith because of the importance I attach to reason. I wanted to reassure you about this. My faith in God is firm as rock. *Ipsa fides non vi, sed ratione, venit.* Faith does not come by force, but by reason. It is *because* I believe that I try to understand and persuade others of the basis of my faith, through those powers of enquiry with which God Himself has blessed me."

Peter's face fell.

This wasn't the sort of confidence he'd been expecting. He was sure it would never have occurred to him to doubt Abelard's faith, and he wondered that such an idea should have troubled him so. But he was nevertheless rather touched that his father should attach such importance to Peter's belief in him as a true Christian. He was able, for the first time, to return Abelard's gaze and say with complete honesty:

"I am sure I would never have doubted that."

This seemed to reassure Abelard, who went on, "And secondly . . ." Peter's face brightened again. ". . . I want you to read with care the verses I have addressed to you and left with your Aunt Denise. The advice in them will help to guide you through adversity. Read the Holy Scriptures, Astralabe, my son, and be governed always by the fear and love of God – despising God is the only real sin.

"Remember that the greatest gift which God can bestow is a true friend, a rare and precious thing. And, bearing in mind the natural impulses of your youth, know that nothing can devour a human mind more completely than a woman, so beware of being driven by wanton desire disguised as love."

Peter nodded dumbly, this time his eyes fixed firmly on Peggy's twitching ears. The track had branched away from the riverbank towards a small wood of evergreens and beech in the final approach to the Angers road. Hugh, some way ahead by now, looked round and waited for them.

"There is, in fact, one more thing." Abelard spoke urgently now, lowering his tone as if in conspiracy.

"The Paraclete, Peter. Before you are much older it is right, I think, that you should make the journey across France to the abbey of the Paraclete. I called it that when we built the first oratory there, from mud and river rushes, because it means the Holy Spirit, the Comforter. That was a time of the most acute grief and sorrow for me which you may read about in the *Historia Calamitatum*, the account of my misfortunes. I've left a copy with Denise. And when you go" – they had nearly caught the others up, and Peter's heart was beating fast for he was afraid they would rejoin them before Abelard had finished – " when the time is right to go, take with you the finished *Planctus*, the laments we spoke of the other day. Yes, it's right you should do that," he added, as if reassuring himself on the point.

The hope that had flickered again in Peter's wide grey eyes died; what he had been half-expecting he didn't really know, but it was more than this after-thought of a command. And yet – it was the only time that Abelard had made explicit a connection between Peter and that third person to and through whom they were both so inextricably linked. It was, he under-stood, a sort of concession, an offering. Not much of one, perhaps, but an offering all the same.

Abelard's final farewell was shared between Peter and Charles.

"Charles, I will write as I promised to my old friend Geoffrey of Chartres about your studies there – I know he'll do what he can to help you find good lodgings and hear the best teachers. God keep you both and guide you in all you do." Peter bowed a respectful fare-well, and noticed how his father shivered as a fresh gust of wind scattered the little party with beech leaves.

Porcarius leant over and touched his nephew on the shoulder: "I'm expecting you to play that rebec like an angel by the time I come back at Christmas!"

"I'll try, Uncle Porcarius – and a thousand times thank you."

"Take good care of your mother, Charles – and remember Lambert," called Hugh, the only one to glance back as they finally parted company.

For a few moments Charles and Peter stood in silence looking after the retreating figures. The beeches burned, as if in passionate revolt against the sombre changeless green of the conifers.

"Part kindly from him, Master Peter – you may not meet again," Maud had said; Maud, who could see into the future.

Eventually Charles said, "*What* a mind!" He shook his head in wonder. "How I would love to be taught by him in Paris – the atmosphere among his students there must be so exciting."

"Mmm." Peter was non-committal. Charles looked at his cousin curiously.

"What do you feel about it all now, Peter?" It didn't occur to him, with his open, straightforward temperament, that Peter might need time before he could answer that question for himself, let alone for anyone else.

Peter shrugged and turned Peggy back in the direction of the Sanguèze.

"I don't know, Charles. Honestly, I don't know."

Charles looked puzzled.

"You didn't *say* much to each other. I mean, I tried to make it easier – on that ride round the estate on the first morning, for instance."

"I know, Charles, I know."

Absurdly, he almost felt he needed to apologize to Charles that his efforts had been in vain.

"Was it *so* difficult for you?"

Peter didn't answer for a few moments. Then he nodded and said, "Yes, the whole thing was a huge ordeal, if you must know. It was something I'd longed for and dreaded all at the same time – and when it eventually happened it was just – well, a disappointment."

"*Disappointment*! How could a man of that magnetism, that brilliance, those looks even – how could he be disappointing? Peter, I've never really understood you – I mean, the way you never seemed to want to talk or know about your parents when Mother or I tried to bring the subject up. It used to puzzle me – and now you say you're disappointed, I'm more puzzled than ever."

Peter, who knew in his heart that Charles genuinely wanted to understand, and that there was no malice in his remarks, was nevertheless irritated. So he hadn't been ready to talk about his parents just because Charles and Denise had happened to think it was the right time. And now he was disappointed. Yes, *disappointed*. Was that so sinful? Why did it have to be his fault, this sense of being let down? Why did everything have to be *his* fault? Did he not have some justification, for all Abelard's magnetism, brilliance and good looks?

But why should he have to explain himself? It was really no business of Charles. Well, he wouldn't explain himself.

"Race you to the ford," he challenged instead, urging Peggy into a brisk canter. Charles pounded after him, shaking his head in perplexity. He was fond of his younger cousin, but sometimes his moods and reactions were just too exasperating for words.

That evening the wind grew stronger still, blowing smoke in little billows down the chimney into the Hall. Ralph, sitting as usual too close to it, had one of his coughing fits and Raoul, who was due to leave the following day, took him away to the far corner to help him with some reading practice. He was the only person patient enough to spend time teaching Ralph, who was so much slower than the three older boys. Charles, on Hugh's instruction, had ridden down to visit Lambert, in one last attempt to persuade him to have the gangrenous leg amputated – something the terrified ploughman was still vehemently resisting.

Peter, enjoying the peace and quiet, was at the opposite end of the Hall from Ralph and Raoul, experimenting quietly with his new Mozarabic rebec. He was just beginning to master the technique of plucking the drone string rhythmically with his thumb, at the same time as plucking a tune on the melody strings with his fingers, when a voice called softly, "Master Peter."

He looked up, to see Nicolette's anxious face in the doorway to the north stair.

"Nicolette!" he said, immediately laying aside the instrument. His heart leapt inside him, and sent the blood singing round his body.

She said breathlessly, "Master Peter – my lady Denise is so sore distressed, I thought I should fetch help. I heard a strange sound in the solar, and when I went to see what it was, the door was open and she was trying to read something, but couldn't because of the sobs which were shaking her."

Denise had been so kind and strong when Nicolette had lost her mother that to see her in this state was almost frightening to the orphaned girl. She looked earnestly at Peter. "*Please* go and see if you can do anything. I . . . I don't like to disturb her."

He rose and put his hands gently on Nicolette's arms. The impulse to kiss the tiny arrow-head birthmark and the line where her dark hair was pulled back from the smooth forehead was intense. But he said reassuringly, "Don't worry. I'll go straightaway."

Within a minute he was knocking on the half-open

door of the solar above, and entering without waiting for a reply.

His Aunt Denise sat in tears beside a low and spluttering fire. She had spread a goatskin from the bedchamber over the rushes and on it, in some disorder, lay a little pile of documents. She was holding one close up to her eyes, a lighted candle in her other hand, as she tried with obvious difficulty to decipher the script.

"Aunt Denise?"

She started when she realized she was no longer alone, but made no attempt to wipe away the tears which ran freely down her cheeks. Her flyaway lock of hair had been joined by others.

"Peter!" she half-sobbed.

In a second Peter was on his knees beside her, taking the candle from her hand and putting his other arm around her shoulders.

"Aunt Denise! What's troubling you so?"

She gestured to the pieces of parchment lying around her and to the one in her hand, and shook her head. Eventually she managed to whisper:

"The letters – between Heloise and Abelard." Gently he took the manuscript from her, afraid that her tears would dissolve the ink.

She went on, "That poor sweet child – I can see her now, refusing to cry out in the pains of childbirth. But *these* cries . . . Oh Peter, the mother in me would like to spare you this, but the woman in me urges you to read them."

Peter looked at her curiously; for him Denise was all mother, and he did not at all care to think of the woman in her. He didn't really understand what she meant anyway.

"I can't even read all the Latin, so what power must they have when they are read properly?"

Peter, his arm still around her shoulders, looked at the offending documents as one might look at an ugly insect or snake, with a blend of fascination and fear.

Surely it would all be there, all the things he had wanted to understand yet never dared to ask. All the things his father had seemed unable to put into words when they met face to face after so many years. And yet – now that they were there in front of him, did he really want them? Almost in spite of himself he began to decipher the Latin in Heloise's clear, bold hand – for it was her originals, together with Thibault's copies of Abelard's replies, which were to be kept at Le Pallet.

'Why, after our entry into religion, which was your decision alone, have I been so neglected and forgotten by you that I have neither a word from you when you are here to give me strength nor the consolation of a letter in absence? Tell me, I say, if you can – or I will tell you what I think and indeed the world suspects. It was desire, not affection which bound you to me, the flame of lust rather than love. So when the end came to what you desired, any show of feeling you used to make went with it. This is not merely my own opinion, beloved, it is everyone's.'

Could it then be true that his father had felt only wanton lust for his mother? Peter felt a shiver of revulsion pass through his body. If that were so, it would help to explain why Abelard had come, according to Porcarius, to accept his mutilation so readily as just punishment from God. What was it he had said in farewell, down in the beech copse by the road to Angers? 'Nothing can devour a human mind more completely than a woman, so beware of being driven by wanton desire in the guise of love.'

It had never occurred to Peter that Heloise might also feel deserted, discarded by Abelard, but the evidence of that now stood stark before him. 'If only your love had less confidence in me, my dear, so that you would be more concerned on my behalf! But as it is, the more I have made you feel secure in me, the more I have to bear with your neglect.' He found the language reasonably easy to follow; perhaps all that study and learning by heart had been of value after all.

And here it was again, that disturbing difference between love and lust, as if the two were at war with one another instead of belonging to each other. If that terrible thing that had been done to Abelard should, God only forbid, ever happen to him, there was no doubt whatsoever, was there, that he would still adore Nicolette? But that didn't mean, if he desired to sleep with her now – even if it were morally wrong according to Abelard's morality of intention – that he didn't really *love* her. Did it? His mother Heloise seemed to have experienced the two-in-one love: 'While I enjoyed with you the pleasures of the flesh, many were uncertain whether I was prompted by love or lust; but now the end is proof of the beginning. I have finally denied myself every pleasure in obedience to your will . . .'

"She has written all this *fifteen years* afterwards – that's what's so heartbreaking," said Denise, still in an awed half-whisper. "I don't understand a lot of it, but I understand this. Listen! 'My heart was not in me but with you, and now, even more, if it is not with you it is nowhere; truly, without you it cannot exist.' *Fifteen* years, Peter, fifteen years."

What was it Maud had said? 'Too sad and too beautiful to forget.' If the old woman's words had been the first to tell him that his mother had suffered in her own right, it was by the power of Heloise's own written word that her ghost, the grey, formless ghost which had haunted him for so long, now moved out of shadow into the soft light of pity.

When Charles appeared in the doorway, he was confronted with the endearing picture of his cousin and mother sitting close together on the floor, their heads bowed over the script of Heloise's second letter.

Leaning over them he asked, "Can I help?"

"Oh yes, Charles. Peter's doing very well but we need help in translating these letters which Abelard has left. I think we may need Raoul up here too, when we come to the long account of Abelards."

"I'm afraid Ralph is coughing badly because of the smoke, but he's refusing to go to his room until Peter goes with him. Louis has been talking to him about ghosts and now he's terrified of being alone in the dark."

"I'm going. I've had enough anyway." Peter got up abruptly and Denise looked at him in surprise. He touched her shoulder gently: "I'd like to read the rest tomorrow, if I may." Now he badly felt the need to be alone again. He understood that Denise wanted help – he himself might have been able to give it to her if he'd trusted himself to read out loud to her – but these private, intimate letters were suddenly becoming too public, and he didn't want to share them any more.

Running down the narrow spiral stairway in the dark, at the bottom he all but knocked over Nicolette who was carrying some milk up to the girls' turret-room. The beaker went flying, Nicolette gave a cry of surprise and, before he knew what was happening, Peter had enfolded her in his arms. He felt the softness of her breasts as, crushed against him, she seemed just for a moment to yield to his embrace; then, almost immediately, she was pulling away, pushing at his chest with her hands, turning away her face which showed paler than ever in the darkness of the stairwell.

"No, no, Master Peter," she whispered, with panic.

"Why not, Nicolette? Why not? I love you. I only

141

want to show you how I love you . . . I won't hurt you," he said urgently, almost dizzy with desire, terrified of rebuff.

"*Please*, Master Peter." She pushed at her hair which, without her usual headdress, was quite dishevelled. "You've always been so kind – I think of you as . . . as a brother. Don't spoil that now, I beseech you."

The fire of the moment was extinguished by those few words 'as a brother'. So that was it. The smiles, the little confidences, the friendly exchanges had all been because she needed a brother and thought she had found one in the gullible, soft-hearted foster-child of her lady employer. Well, he didn't like it that way at all. Indeed, he found it insulting. He didn't need any more sisters in his life, that was certain. If she didn't want him as a young man, with all his desire and devotion, she could have none of him. Not that she'd care about that – he probably wasn't worth having anyway, as lover or brother.

He stood aside and bowed a formal little bow.

"Please pass. I'm sorry to have detained you."

"Master *Peter*." Her country accent was more noticeable than usual. She seemed genuinely distressed: "I had no wish to hurt you. But such things cannot be between us."

"As you wish."

"Don't you understand?"

"No."

"I am but a servant of your aunt, my lady Denise."

"Then, as a servant, how can I be your brother?" And he thought, she's lying, of course. If she had any feeling for me her position in the household would have no bearing on the matter. Everyone knows that even kings take lovers from among their servants – hadn't William, Conqueror of England, been the bastard son of a tanner's daughter? Besides, there was no such gap in this case. Had her grandfather not run the estate almost single-handed in the old days, when *his* grandfather, Sir Berengar, was away from home? And had not his father, the great Peter Abelard, seen fit to conduct *her* grandfather's funeral service? No, there was some other reason. Either she simply didn't like him – or there was someone else.

"Is it Fulk?" he asked sullenly, yet almost hoping that it was.

"Oh *Fulk*!" she laughed, with a sort of affectionate dismissal.

"I see. He's another brother, is he?" Peter was half-relieved, half-disturbed by her reaction. Fulk was obviously not a serious rival, yet as a rival he, at least, would not have been so very formidable.

She ignored the question.

"Let it just be as it was." She laid a hand on his arm, and looked up at him in the dim light that filtered through the open doorway from the Hall. Her voice was so pleading, she seemed so genuinely to want to restore their friendship that he began, just a little, to relent. How, after all, could he resist? If he were to keep this little bit of her for himself he must – for the time being – relinquish the rest.

"I'm sorry," he said softly. He leant down to pick up the fallen beaker and held it into what light there was.

"Not much use now, I'm afraid – it's badly cracked." But he handed it back to her all the same, and she thanked him, politely, without meeting his gaze.

## 13

Somehow Peter got through that night. He lay for hours, his hands behind his head, staring at the few stars which hung imprisoned in the black frame of the arrow-slit window. Sleep overpowered him, though, before he could witness their stealthy release by daylight.

He was saved from too much brooding the following day by the appearance of Denis, the older of Lambert's two sons, a good deal less impudent and full of himself than usual.

"Can I speak with Master Charles, please?"

Charles appeared behind Peter at the top of the steps in the doorway to the Great Hall, eating a piece of bread and cheese.

"What is it, Denis? Does your father want to see me again?"

"He's changed his mind, Master Charles. He'll have the leg off – but Mother sent me to beg you to arrange it as quickly as possible, before he changes his mind again." The boy's voice grew faint: "It's hell in our hut at the moment."

Under his eyes large dark rings had recently appeared, and Peter guessed that the boy was getting very little sleep.

"Come in and eat something," he said kindly.

"Thank you, Master Peter, but Mother told me I was to hurry back with your answer. Father's in such a state."

"I'm afraid I didn't help much last night," said Charles slowly, finishing his bread. He turned to Peter. "I told him his choice was either to live with one leg or die – very soon – with two."

"It's only what we've been telling him for days, but it sounded different when you said it. He's that afraid." Peter noticed that the boy seemed older and slower as a result of the family's ordeal. He imagined the interior of the ploughman's hut, hot and heavy with the smell of disease and fear, and for a few moments he actually forgot his parents' letters, forgot even Nicolette and her rebuff.

"It's not surprising he's afraid – after all, it's not so long ago that poor old Goosefoot had his amputation and everyone knows what happened to him." Goosefoot had been the village thatcher and after a bad fall had allowed his leg to be amputated by a travelling quack. The operation had gone horribly wrong, the marrow had burst and the poor man had died in an agony which Maud's best efforts at anaesthetic – a brew of hemlock, mulberry juice, ivy and mandrake – had done nothing to assuage. Charles frowned at his cousin, who immediately blushed in dismay. He had meant to make Lambert's terror more understandable, to do away with any idea that he might be a coward, but realized immediately that his reminder of Goosefoot's fate had been less than tactful. Why was he always so clumsy?

Raoul, coming across from the chapel where he'd been at morning prayer, overheard Peter's remarks and became aware there had been a development.

"As I said yesterday, the best thing is for Charles to ride back to Nantes with me now. I know a surgeon who spent several years at the great school in Salerno – if anyone can do the job properly, it will be him."

"But . . ." Denis looked even more worried at this.

145

"Yes, it'll be expensive," said Charles, anticipating the objection because it was something that he knew worried Lambert himself, who was a freeman, not a serf. "Father left instructions that your father should be given the best care – he doesn't like the idea of anyone at Le Pallet dying in agony, Denis, you should know that." The note of pride in Charles's voice was clear.

Denis mumbled some thanks and ran off. Charles, Peter and Raoul watched as, passing the stable door, little Philippe trotted eagerly towards him. Denis meted out a rough sideways kick instead of a greeting; the younger boy recoiled in pain and looked after him in bewilderment, the smile on his moon-shaped face fading only slowly.

The Salerno-trained surgeon was duly located and brought back from Nantes by noon on the following day. In the meantime Denise and Peter sat in shifts with the frightened patient and his family, for there was no question, at his advanced stage of disease, of bringing him up to the house. Maud came but was turned away, for Lambert's wife was one of the villagers who mistrusted her most, and everyone knew she'd not been able to do anything to help Goosefoot. Many of the other villagers came as well, bearing little gifts – grapes from Guillaume, three duck eggs, apple cheese, a partridge shot clean by Fulk with his bow and arrow – but they all remained outside the hut. Only Peter, Charles and 'the lady Denise' were allowed the dubious privilege of entry – and the pale diffident priest for a few moments about twice a day. When the two redhead sons, who were about eleven and twelve, were sent away to another cottage, Peter knew with sickening certainty that he would be expected to assist at the operation itself.

The surgeon – an exceptionally tall man who had to stoop low to enter the hut – wrinkled his nose as he did

146

so. He scattered some scented solution liberally in an attempt to drown the stench of putrefaction. Charles, watching from the doorway where the surgeon had handed him his cloak, couldn't help wondering if this artificial masking scent was going to add much to the cost of the whole thing. He wished, not for the first time, that his father had been there, especially as the surgeon had assured him on the way back from Nantes that the astrological signs were not at all auspicious that week for an operation on a man born in Capricorn.

Peter, wiping the sick man's forehead as he had twenty times in the past hour, watched the grisly iron instruments becoming red hot as the physician heated them in the fire in the middle of the floor.

Lambert clutched at Peter's wrist with the ferocity of a wild beast. "Don't go," he whispered in a scarcely human voice.

"No, I won't go," reassured Peter. But even as he saw and pitied the terror in the man's eyes, part of him did – had to – go. In his mind he escaped the sweltering confines of the hut as if to hover somewhere above. In a strangely detached way, he compared the anguish which lay sweating on the straw mattress beside him with Heloise's loneliness, and the despair he himself had experienced in the north stairwell, when Nicolette had pushed herself out of his embrace. If such comparisons were sinful, he didn't feel them to be so. He felt only wonder at the amount of misery which God could tolerate in His world, and yet also a new understanding of why Abelard had, in the midst of his own torment, founded a refuge called the Paraclete – the Holy Spirit, the Comforter.

The command came for Lambert's wife, Charles and himself to hold the ploughman firmly, each by one limb. Then everything happened very quickly. The surgeon handed Peter a small sponge, soaked in some herbal solution, and told him to hold it close up to the man's nose.

"Breathe deeply," ordered the surgeon, "and turn your head to the right."

"Breathe deeply," echoed Peter, his stomach heaving with dread at what he was about to see. With one hand he held on very tightly to Lambert's right arm, while trying with the other to keep the sponge steady immediately in front of his nostrils. When the urge to drop Lambert's wrist and rush in panic for the doorway threatened to be too great for him to resist, he thought of Nicolette and how her eyes might for a moment cease laughing and fill with admiration when she heard of the vital part he had played.

And when the feral howl of anguish actually came, though he held on tight as instructed by the surgeon, Peter's eyes closed in a grimace of such force that his lips laid bare the full length of his gums and a voice inside him shrieked: 'Nicolette, this is for you – see what I can do!'

Afterwards, as Lambert sank into a merciful oblivion and the surgeon handed Peter another solution – this time of fennel juice – to bring him round, Peter did manage to mutter a fervent prayer for the mutilated man and his wife, whose eyes were fixed in horror on the severed limb as it lay bleeding and suppurating on the mud floor. He looked across at Charles, whose usually florid face was paler than Peter had ever seen it before and shone with sweat. All at once the hellish mixture of stifling heat, of fear and pain, of the smell of the patient's rotting flesh overpowered him. He rushed to the doorway only just in time before vomiting violently all over the path.

The surgeon, who was of course given hospitality at the manor-house, had to be suitably entertained over

148

the next few days between visits to the patient who, against all the auspices according to the learned expert, soon began to show signs of progress. For Peter and Charles this meant a hawking expedition and several accompanied visits to a new eel-trap in the mill-race, as well as polite and apparently endless participation in chess, at which the distinguished visitor was keen to show his skill. "I carry my own pieces with me – I feel more comfortable playing with them," he said, showing Charles and Peter the exquisite ivory set he had brought back from Salerno in southern Italy.

And so a little while elapsed before Peter was able to think about asking Denise if he could have access again to his parents' correspondence. But it was precisely this that was on his mind as, later in the afternoon of the surgeon's departure, he made his way up from the ploughman's hut towards the house. As he approached the orchard crossway he saw Nicolette coming towards him, a basket under one arm.

He had not seen her alone since the scene on the north stair and so, effectively disguising the little surge of joy which always rose in him at the sight of her, he asked matter-of-factly where she was going.

"Berthe asked me to fetch the goat's cheese from Thérèse and honey while I'm there from Herluin next door."

Peter made a face. Berthe loved sending people on what should have been her own errands.

"No, it's all right – I always like going to see Thérèse and the boys," smiled Nicolette, understanding his look. "But how is Lambert? You look tired, Master Peter."

It's your love I want, not your pity, thought Peter morosely. But, as always, he was won over by her smile, which this time was also one of genuine concern.

"Well, I've not had much sleep recently. Aunt

Denise wanted either Charles or me to stay down with Lambert's wife until he was out of danger." Peter passed his hand across his eyes and through his hair, aware for the first time that Nicolette was right and that he was, indeed, very tired. He looked down at her and was just wondering if he might ask to accompany her to Thérèse's, when she darted a sudden wide-eyed look over his shoulder and patches of pink appeared in her cheeks. At the same moment he heard the thud of hooves. Almost before he had wheeled around to discover whose approach could have had such an effect on her, he knew what he was going to see. And he was right. Towards them, on the path leading from the river, came his Uncle Hugh on his black palfrey, Noblesse, while beside him on Esprit, the horse's magnificent bay coat gleaming in the late afternoon sun, rode Louis, upright and elegant as ever. Without acknowledging them, Peter turned back to Nicolette, whose open expressive face and shining eyes concealed nothing.

After a moment's hesitation, she said, "I – I must go for the cheese. Until later, Master Peter." He stood looking after her, but without seeing her quickly retreating figure; he saw only the surprise and joy which had irradiated her face at his cousin Louis's unexpected return. He turned, as courtesy demanded, to walk towards the riders with a welcoming wave of his hand – and murder in his heart.

It was as much as Peter could do to sit through the evening meal, listening to plans for Louis's forthcoming placement as squire in the County of Anjou, for the brief visit had gone well and Hugh was pleased with the knight who was to be Louis's master for the next few years. Whenever Peter glanced down the long table at Nicolette, she was busying herself with either Agatha or Agnes, hiding her secret well.

150

It was a relief when Denise said, "I think Charles and Peter should retire early – you've had very little sleep these past few nights."

"Yes, you've carried out your responsibilities with great credit. I'm proud of you both," said Hugh in his slow, formal manner. Denise had told him what had happened in selected detail, leaving out the bit about Peter's attack of vomiting.

"The action *would* all happen while I was away," complained Louis, with a note of real envy in his voice. There was a silence around the table, for no one knew how to answer such a remark; Peter thought back to Lambert's howl at the moment of severance and felt only contempt for his cousin's thirst for action at any price. He looked down at Nicolette, sure, for once, of an instant of triumph – but she was cutting up something for Agnes, with whom she shared a plate, and gave nothing away.

For Peter the salt pork and river fish and fruit and fresh milk suddenly tasted sour. As he sat there listening to Louis's plans, and thinking of Charles's approaching departure for the cathedral school in Chartres, he realized that there was little to keep him at Le Pallet either. He didn't want to be anyone's squire, always at their beck and call, only to become a knight eternally at the service of the local overlord, as Hugh was for part of every year to Fat Conan of Brittany. He wanted to devote himself to making music and he certainly couldn't do that on a remote country estate. And Nicolette clearly didn't want him, so what was there to detain him here? He would go to the abbey of the Paraclete, as Abelard had proposed. Not in two years, not next year, but soon – now, even. For the first time in his life he would turn to his mother, Heloise, for comfort and guidance. All the omens were there: Abelard's unexpected visit, the sudden appearance of

151

the letters, Nicolette's rejection and now Louis's obvious place in her affections. It was time to go – to the sanctuary of the Holy Spirit, the Comforter.

But first he had to know what was written about him in the rest of the correspondence, what feelings his parents had had at the time of parting with him, what decisions they had made. It was strange, perhaps, that there had been no mention of him in Heloise's two letters, but no doubt that would be explained by Abelard's actual account of the events as they had happened. The knowledge and understanding that that would give him would surely help him to face his stranger-mother. So, emboldened by this new resolve, Peter sought out his aunt after the meal and asked to see again the documents they had begun to decipher together, with Denise in tears beside the fire. At first reluctant to let them out of safekeeping in the solar, she quickly understood that his politely worded request covered an urgent command. And besides, she reflected, are they not in truth more his than mine?

"Just take one at a time," she pleaded, "for safety's sake. Start with Abelard's account of his misfortunes. That's in the smallest leather pouch, on top of the others. And Peter – don't be too late to sleep tonight."

It was with great eagerness, though without really knowing what it was he expected, that Peter took the record of his father's life and perched himself with it on the window embrasure in his turret room. No longer aware of exhaustion, he read with the help of moon and candle and despite the interference of numerous insects, until he heard Ralph wheezing on his way up the spiral stairs. He'd finish it tomorrow, he thought, though not with great confidence as his progress in Abelard's advanced Latin was slow and he was forced to skip several passages. But he had now reached the part where Abelard the young man, after making enemies at the school in Laon, had returned to Paris to begin rebuilding his wealth and fame as a teacher in the capital. At any moment, Peter realized, Heloise would appear in the story. And soon would come the crucial part which related to him, which, in some as yet unformulated way, would surely help or guide him on his way to the Paraclete.

And, in an unexpected way, this is exactly what happened.

## 14

Peter woke at first light feeling, for the first time in days, a sense of pleasant anticipation. Eagerly he pushed off the goatskin cover, dressed swiftly and put on his cloak against the autumn chill which had crept through the very stones of the turret wall. Stopping only to cover Ralph more adequately as he lay on his back breathing noisily through his mouth, Peter picked up the leather pouch containing Abelard's manuscript and made his way quietly up the winding stairway, past the little room where he'd been born, to the parapet at the top of the tower. Outside the ground lay obscured in a grey mist so that the old beech tree sagging in its corner of the courtyard appeared to be floating, eerie and rootless. Peter crouched in the shelter of the tower and drew his cloak more closely round him before opening the manuscript.

Such was his haste to reach the part which referred to him that he glossed forgivingly over the bald admission that Abelard had set out to seduce the very much younger Heloise 'confident that I should have an easy success'. Likening her to a tender lamb, himself to a ravening wolf, he wrote at first in the language of desire; but it was obvious that desire soon became tempered by love and tenderness (again those two 'opposite' faces of love, Peter thought) and then, after the discovery of their affair by Heloise's uncle, the bit he'd been waiting for: 'Soon afterwards the girl found that she was pregnant, and immediately wrote me a letter full of rejoicing to ask what I thought she should do.' Peter re-read the lines, tracing the word 'rejoicing' with his finger to make sure he had made no mistake. 'One night then, when her uncle was away from home, I removed her secretly from his house, as we had planned, and sent her straight to my own country. There she stayed with my sister until she gave birth to a boy, whom she called Astralabe.'

Frowning with intense concentration Peter read on, sometimes poring over sentences two or even three times to ensure he understood them properly. No more mention of the baby, of him, at this point: obviously it would come a little later. The account switched to the reaction of Heloise's uncle and to the decision of Abelard to marry the girl he had wronged. After ascertaining that a marriage would appease the uncle, Abelard had set off again for Brittany. But he had not expected the vehemence of Heloise's reaction to his proposal of marriage. Peter remembered how Porcarius had tried to explain Heloise's reluctance to marry Abelard, but he still didn't really understand either the point or the power of the arguments which she borrowed from such distant figures as St Jerome and Cicero. Abelard had recalled and recorded them here in his account, and in detail. Cicero, for example, had refused to marry again, after his divorce, because he couldn't 'devote his attention to a wife and philosophy alike'. Peter shook his head in perplexity and glanced up for a moment's break. He couldn't have known, but he actually sat very close to the spot where Heloise had argued at her most passionate – that too had been an early morning. But he paused only for a moment. Suddenly he was reading objections put forward by Heloise which had nothing to do with Cicero or any other ancient sage. Suddenly she was referring to other evils brought about by marriage, to the inconvenience

155

and disturbance caused by babies and children, to – why did she not admit it? – the evil that was *him*. 'Who can concentrate on thoughts of scripture or philosophy and be able to endure babies crying . . . will he put up with the constant muddle and squalor which small children bring into the home?' Was this the same young woman who, according to Abelard, had rejoiced to find herself with child? If, only months, maybe just weeks – for Abelard did not make the timing clear – after the birth of that child she could talk about children in such disparaging terms, then what a monumental disappointment he must have been to her.

He stopped reading and looked around, distraught, as if searching for comfort. But the golden fingers of light which had begun to soften and break up the dough-like mist were indifferent to him, and there was no comfort in the patches of grass which now lay revealed on Cow Common, shining in a film of dew.

He forced himself then to read how Heloise's frantic efforts at dissuasion had made no impression on Abelard's obstinate intention to marry her, and how, like a star at daybreak, he, their son, had simply faded out of their story: 'And so when our baby son was born we entrusted him to my sister's care and returned secretly to Paris.' Nothing more. His birth seemed to have had no effect on them at all. He read on, still with a glimmer of hope, until Heloise publicly bound herself to the religious life, after the attack on Abelard. 'Heloise had already agreed to take the veil in obedience to my wishes and entered a convent.' The bald statements enraged him as they had when Porcarius first told him the story: how *could* he wish such a thing, how *could* she obey?

No, there really was nothing more. No discussion about whether to give him up, no thoughts about his upbringing or his future, nothing about contact with either of his parents – *nothing*. Just as there had been nothing in Heloise's letters about her lost motherhood. Well, he wouldn't bother to look at those again – they were as irrelevant to him as he had obviously been to her. The script which had promised so much now scowled up at him; in rage he tore at the parchment, desperate to destroy the evidence of what, he realized now, he had dimly suspected for a long time. But it was tough and resisted him so that he made only a small incision at the top of a page. The effort, like his entire existence, was pathetic, of no significance at all. Was there any wonder that Nicolette didn't love him if his own mother had seen him merely as the creator of muddle and squalor? He heard again the cithara music of Michaelmas night when the pilgrims had returned, and saw Nicolette's dark eyes laughing at him before they were obscured by Louis's shoulders – except that now, instead of laughing merrily, they teased and taunted. He saw again the joy on her face at the early arrival of Louis resplendent on his fine horse, and he felt her hands pushing against his own chest in rejection.

Crumpling the manuscript roughly inside his shirt, Peter got up then and rushed down the turret stairs. Ignoring Berthe who – too startled for sarcasm – was drawing the first bucket from the well, he ran across to the stables. Thomas wasn't yet up and little Philippe was still curled in his usual foetal position in the straw. Within minutes Peggy was bridled and Peter was riding her out of the courtyard, with only a couple of barking hounds to complain. He didn't know where he was going, only that he had to get out and away. At first the pony threw up her head in her habit of protest, but seemed appeased when Peter leant forward, flat against her mane, and whispered into the comforting warmth of her neck. He rode through the dew-sodden grass of the meadows, then up onto Boundary Ridge and towards the western edge which looked out over the village and valley. At once comforted and irritated by the familiarity of the scene, he watched as wisps of smoke coiled from the holes in the cottage roofs and Thérèse, far below, led her goats to Cow Common. He looked up into the now clear sky and cried out loud:

"Oh God, if my poor life is worth the sacrifice of Your Son, Jesus Christ, show me what I should do. My father Abelard the eunuch has told me to visit my mother, his holy whore, yet her words are surely witness to the fact that she has no thought of me. I want to go, I dread to go – so guide me, God." The prayer was a blend of supplication and the worst sacrilege of which he was capable – to insult one's parents was sinful enough, to offer that insult in prayer to God was as evil as blasphemy.

He turned Peggy back into the east wind and kicked her into a canter along the top of the ridge, where he had so often raced with his cousins and Robert's sons. The canter quickly became a gallop and Peter laughed with the harsh jubilation of speed; "Father eunuch, Mother whore," he cried into the wind, attempting to set the words in ever more glorious profanity to the tune of his father's hymn.

Suddenly, just as they drew near the tall hedgerow where the bloodberries grew, a hare dashed out of its cover, no doubt startled by Peter's cries. Peggy shied in alarm and came to an abrupt halt. Peter had no chance at all of remaining on her back; he fell awkwardly and landed, with a dull thud, on his head.

When he came to, Peggy was nuzzling him gently, for once uncertain how to react. He lay very still for a while, watching little white clouds glide high against the blue, noticing the grey tangles of old man's beard which had replaced honeysuckle in the hedge. Everything seemed extraordinarily clear, like after rain. He felt Peggy's warm breath and the soft dampness of her muzzle. Gradually he began to test his fingers, his feet, his arms, his legs, his head – which seemed much heavier than it had before. He had no recollection of what had caused the fall, but remembered only his headlong flight to destruction, that dreadful calumny on his lips.

"Peggy, I'm alive, I'm saved," he whispered, incredulously – and was overwhelmed by a sudden sense of well-being. "I was punished for my sin, Peggy, but I'm *saved*. My life is precious after all." Gingerly he got to his feet again and put his arms round the pony's neck; tears seeped into the coarse grey hairs, but they were tears not of despair but of relief, thanksgiving and penitence. His head ached, his arms ached, his back ached; but his heart was light with a new confidence. It didn't occur to him not to mount again immediately, such had been his training since early childhood.

He did so slowly, with discomfort, confiding out loud to his uncritical companion, "I *will* go to the Paraclete, that is surely the sign, Peggy." And, for himself in silence, he added, "After all, I've got a lot of things to take with me. And *she*'s the only one who can help."

Denise was not surprised by Peter's bruised and bedraggled appearance that morning; indeed she had scarcely slept after lending him Abelard's manuscript. Charles had given her more help with the documents while Peter had sat with Lambert one night, and she herself had felt surprise and pain, on Peter's behalf, that he was so glaringly absent from the writings. And anger. She'd known again the anger which had flared up in Abelard's presence, and now, for the first time, felt glad that it had. When Peter announced, calmly and simply, that he intended to visit the Paraclete very soon – and alone if necessary – she accepted the statement without objection, and just sent him off to the kitchens where Berthe, with a surprising lack of complaint, set a tub of herb-strewn water to heat for bathing the bruises. Denise, meanwhile, spent the rest of the day worrying about how the journey could be accomplished – in her view it was unthinkable that a boy not yet fully sixteen should travel across France with no more than a servant for company.

Later that evening she broached the subject with Hugh.

"Denise, I've told you, I cannot spare any more time away from the estate, not until Guillaume is accustomed to his new duties as steward. I fear there may be some trouble over that with Bernard."

"Surely not. Everyone at Le Pallet loves Guillaume."

"Maybe. But Bernard has been a good hayward for years and I know he's ambitious. And there's Raymond, too. He's disgruntled because we haven't done much hawking this year. But apart from all that, I've spent too long away already and it'll soon be time to do my month's fee for the Count again. Peter will have to wait until the New Year, when Louis leaves. Then I could take him to the Paraclete and combine it with the fair at Provins perhaps. I may even have to go there for the Count."

"He needs to go now, Hugh. That fall this morning . . . next time he may not be so lucky."

"I sincerely hope there won't be a next time. The boy needs to be a great deal more sensible. He's almost a man, now, Denise – you treat him as though he were a young child still. I sometimes think you mother him more than you ever have either Charles or Louis."

"Perhaps," she acknowledged quietly. Charles and Louis have less need of me, she thought to herself. But she said nothing more, for she recognized the growing irritation in her husband's tone, and had no wish to make it worse. She would clearly have to think of something else. If only she were a man, she could go herself; it would be wonderful to see Heloise again. In many ways. But it wouldn't be the same as the time they had spent together all those years ago, Denise with Charles as a little boy of three and Louis an inquisitive tottering baby, and Heloise with child. Joyfully with child. Or so it had seemed at the time. Denise frowned and shook her head; the absence in the correspondence of any reference to parting with Peter had really quite shocked her. She remembered the moment; Heloise, with tears in her eyes but a firm voice, had handed her the little bundle and said:

"Love him well, dear Denise. May God bless you both."

At the time there had seemed nothing strange about the brevity of the parting. There had been no indication that it would be so final, though Heloise had made no secret of the fact that she was returning to Paris to marry Abelard with deep foreboding that things would not go well for them. "We shall both be destroyed," Heloise had said prophetically to Abelard. "All that is left us is suffering as great as our love has been." If only I understood, thought Denise, as she tried to mend a tear in Ralph's tunic, why she didn't return here when Abelard was injured, instead of taking up the religious life. Surely he would have come to accept that she was only doing her maternal duty, that she was no less loyal to him. They say she's famous and revered as an abbess, but it's quite obvious she didn't really have the heart for it. What a sacrifice. I feel such pity for her – she was such a special child – yet there is a part of me which condemns her, too.

Plunged in these thoughts, Denise was unaware that her lips were moving.

Hugh called to her softly, "What are you muttering

161

to yourself, dearest? Come – it's late. How many tunics has Ralph ruined this year?"

The next day a messenger arrived with a letter which was to solve the problem. The letter was for Charles from Geoffrey of Chartres; Abelard had not even had to write to him as he'd promised, because they'd met unexpectedly at Angers, where Abelard had stayed for a couple of nights with Porcarius to rest the horses. As Abelard had anticipated, his old and loyal friend had immediately pledged to do all he could for Charles – and Peter at a later date if so required – and the letter was accordingly one of welcome. Congenial lodgings could be found with good friends of his, of that 'his mother, the gentle lady Denise, can be assured'. Denise blushed with pleasure; Geoffrey had visited Le Pallet once on his way to Nantes, shortly after the Council of Soissons in 1121, where Abelard was prosecuted for heresy and had to burn his book on the Trinity. Geoffrey had been one of the few to stand by Abelard then, and that, coupled with his handsome face and carriage, had made him a hero in her eyes.

Charles, if taken aback at the unexpectedly speedy arrival of the news, was delighted. He wouldn't have admitted as much, but he was secretly very pleased to be leaving home before Louis. He readily accepted Denise's suggestion that he should first accompany Peter to the Paraclete, and that Peter and a suitable companion – perhaps Fulk – could then return to Le Pallet via a detour to Chartres. Hugh, too, seemed to like the idea; perhaps to make up for his previous lack of co-operation, he even rode down specially to Robert's cottage to ask his permission for Fulk to make the journey. The young man seemed to Hugh and Denise the best choice, for not only was he good-humoured and dependable, but he was also large and strong and would be a good protector should trouble arise on the road. Hugh had once had occasion, unbeknown to his wife, to put this to the test. Robert, who was not finding it easy to teach his skilled craft to his willing but rather clumsy son, was only too happy to oblige, and Fulk himself – his appetite for travel whetted by the pilgrimage to Compostela – was delighted.

But no sooner had the arrangements been made to everyone's satisfaction, than Denise began to fuss and worry. Her anxiety over preparations for the return of Hugh and the other pilgrims from Compostela had been as nothing compared with the frenzy into which the whole household was now thrown. Were the boys really old enough to travel so far in such a small group? Did they have good enough directions? How many clothes should Charles take with him? Should he have his best goatskin blanket? How much money would he need? And which would be the best horses – there was no question of Peter travelling such a long way on that unreliable pony of his. The strong smell of mutton-fat soap filled the courtyard as Berthe and Marie bent over tubs of steaming water scrubbing clothes, deserting the kitchens and condemning the family to cold pork and bread and cheese for what seemed like days on end – until Louis lost patience and went off hawking with Raymond, returning with a hare and three partridges, which he insisted on having cooked 'before everyone loses their wits'.

Denise's loom was pressed into service for the first time since before Agnes was born, and both she and Nicolette spent every spare moment repairing old and making new garments. Peter had no difficulty in avoiding Nicolette, much to his relief for he simply didn't know how to behave with her any more.

The evening before they were due to leave, Peter paid a visit to Maud. She was milking one of the ewes

163

and told him to take a seat on the bench beside the shack. He waited contentedly, watching the willow shadows stretch across the river as the November sun sank quickly behind Boundary Ridge. Suddenly a minute grey creature with a black patch on its face rolled over to expose a miniature abdomen of silky pink, which it clearly felt needed attention of some sort. Peter laughed with delight; still tiny, still weak, and only just walking, Blanche's unwanted puppy was obviously going to survive.

Maud hobbled over to him, her bucket frothing with the warm milk. She smiled.

"Do you see a difference?"

"It's amazing, Maud. A miracle."

"Nonsense. A bit of good care and nourishment, that's all it takes," she said matter-of-factly.

"Agnes'll be so pleased."

"Mmmm." The old woman put down her pail. "Not yet awhile she won't – that dog needs special attention for a good many weeks yet."

Something in her tone made Peter look at her sharply. Maud had always seemed so wise, so self-sufficient. Yet those two silly sheep and the few hens couldn't be much company around that dismal shack, beside the spot in the river where her only daughter had drowned with her unborn baby. It had never really occurred to him before, but for all her keen observations of what other people were feeling, there must, in her own rather quaint words, be a haunting 'song of sadness' in Maud's heart.

"Maud, you don't have to give her back to Agnes, you know. In fact, I think she'd be better off staying here."

"Silly boy – what are you talking about," she muttered, but her wide toothless grin told him that the offer was readily accepted. "Anyway, Guillaume says

164

you and Master Charles are going off on a journey."

"Yes, that's why I'm here. We're taking Charles to study at the school in Chartres, but on the way – well, it's not on the way, you know, but before – we're going to the abbey of the Paraclete to visit . . . Heloise." He wasn't sure whether he'd ever actually used the name out loud to anyone before. It sounded very strange.

"I thought as much." She nodded to herself. "That's how it should be. You'll be sixteen this Christmas-tide if I'm not mistaken. A young man now."

"It doesn't always feel like that." Maud was the only person he could confess that to.

"Well, it takes time. Everything does," she said in her rather slow, enigmatic way. Peter sometimes had the feeling that she knew the secret of the world, and that almost every time she said something she was giving him one more little hint or clue which would lead him nearer to it. Perhaps that's how Arthur's knights had felt in their quest for the Holy Grail, he reflected.

"I've been expecting this," she said, and disappeared for a moment into the hut. When she re-emerged, she handed Peter a little earthenware cask, probably the only one she had, for earthenware was not cheap and she didn't have much to barter with.

"She'll remember old Maud and her special cordial. Take this and tell her – tell her I've thought of her through the years as I've watched her good boy grow to manhood and, if I'm not mistaken, she needs the strength more now than ever she did at Le Pallet."

Peter looked solemnly at the cask and then at Maud; he took it from her with a sense of ceremony and, aware of the strong symbolic value of the gift, said earnestly, "If I were her, I'd be very very pleased."

But I have no idea whether she will be pleased, he thought to himself. He wished he could imagine the scene where he would hand it over, but it was like trying to imagine life in the Holy Land or some other distant country. For between the Peter who stood in that familiar spot in his home valley, and the Peter who would meet and speak to Heloise, abbess of the Paraclete, there stretched a vast uncharted sea.

That evening the family came together in the little chapel to pray for the safe passage of the travellers. As they emerged into the dark courtyard, Denise took Peter's arm.

"Do you remember that really fine wool, the deep blue, which Hugh got in Nantes with some of our cattle-hide last winter? The one I was so pleased with?"

"Ye-es," said Peter, puzzled.

"Well, Nicolette particularly wanted to make your new under-tunic in it. I'd thought she'd want to make something for Fulk, but she was set on using the best cloth and for you." She looked at him keenly in the light of the candle she was carrying. "I didn't know that you and Nicolette . . ."

"There's nothing to know, Aunt Denise. Really. Perhaps there might have been, but she would have none of it. I'm glad about the tunic, though, and I'm glad you told me."

It wasn't that knowing about Nicolette's efforts with the tunic made him feel better about what had happened – or not happened – between them; but it did help in a curious way to prepare him finally for departure. As if, though he couldn't have her love, he at least had her blessing.

## 15

In the commotion of departure next morning, Peter found it easy to exchange a quiet word with Nicolette. He wore the deep-blue under-tunic, its long sleeves fastened at his wrists. The grey over-tunic was in striking contrast and made him look – thought Denise as she tried to see him with the eyes of a stranger – extremely handsome. The most endearing thing about Peter was that, having grown up in the shadow of Louis's dark, more dazzling good looks, he had no idea of the appeal of his own fine sensitive features and slim straight build.

"Aunt Denise told me that I've you to thank for my tunic." He was delighted to see that he'd managed to induce the same patchy little blushes in her cheeks as Louis had when he arrived home unexpectedly and surprised them on the orchard path.

"I wanted to make things right again," she said, looking shyly at the ground. Peter wanted to put out his hand and lift her face so that he could look once more into her eyes. Did she really think that a piece of fine cloth and a few hours' needlework could balance the weight of his unrequited love? There couldn't be much passion in her feelings for Louis if that's what she thought. Maud had said that people's suffering affected them in different ways; perhaps it was the same with falling in love. He wondered if that put him among the lucky, or unlucky, ones. But, all the same, the tunic had given him pleasure, and when she did look up he was smiling at her. Maybe it was the aura of adventure which now surrounded him, but for the first time she thought how handsome he was.

"Farewell – and may God grant you a safe journey and safe return."

Perhaps it was his imminent departure which gave him the confidence, but he leant forward and gave her a chaste little kiss on her forehead – as near the tiny arrow-head blemish as he dared. He smiled his shy friendly smile again and, gesturing with one hand towards the other blue-clad arm, said, "I shan't be able to forget you, shall I?" Before she could reply, he'd turned away to lift Agnes up onto Peggy's back – he had insisted that the pony should be his mount for the journey.

And so, for the second time in less than three weeks, Le Pallet said good-bye to departing members of Lord Hugh's family. Just as before, the travellers were accompanied by a little retinue of well-wishers as far as the ford, where Maud met them bearing three sprigs of mugwort 'to relieve the toil of travelling'. Peter noticed that for the first time she walked with the help of a stick.

"Tell Heloise," said Denise, standing aside with Peter and taking his hand in both of hers, "tell my sister Heloise that I still pray for her every night. In your saddlebag you'll find a little piece of wool cloth – it was white once but it's very grey now and rather threadbare. It's the little blanket you were wrapped in the day she handed you to me. It's served its use, I think." She tried to laugh up at him, wondering if he would think her very silly, but tears shone in her eyes and when she embraced him it was with a fervour she had seldom shown before. Peter realized at that moment just how difficult this all was for Denise. He owed her so much; and whatever welcome awaited

168

him three hundred miles away from his mother in the flesh, it was Denise who would always be mother in his heart. Yet just then he couldn't find the words to tell her so, and was relieved when Charles came over to kiss her farewell.

When Peter looked back from the other side of the river, he didn't this time hesitate to wave. The women stood in a group close together and his wave seemed to acknowledge them all (even Berthe had come this time), but it was Denise – and not Nicolette or anyone else – for whom it was really intended.

They made good progress the first day and stopped at nightfall at a village inn on the road to Angers. Peter was almost immediately singled out for attention by a tavern prostitute somewhere in her mid-thirties, much to Fulk's amusement, Charles's surprise and Peter's own embarrassment – tinged, though he would never have admitted it, with a sense of flattery. She had a certain blowsy appeal and a huge mass of unkempt auburn hair, and so persistently friendly was she – "How I'd love a son just like you, dear," she kept saying in a not at all maternal way – that when it came to settling down for the night in the straw by the fire, Fulk and Charles took it upon themselves to lie one on each side of Peter in order to protect him.

"Some people don't know good fortune when they see it – she'd teach him a thing or two," grinned Fulk, winking at Charles over Peter's head in the wavering light. But Charles did not have the same robust sense of humour as Fulk and his brothers, and only blushed. Someone belched loudly in another corner, and Peter thought nostalgically of the little room in the South Tower, where Ralph would no doubt be snuffling innocently in his sleep.

It was a pleasant relief to arrive in Angers and be

welcomed by Porcarius, who was delighted to see them. They ate good venison and drank wine which tasted different from that made at Le Pallet – probably, explained Porcarius enthusiastically, because it was fermented in barrels no longer lined with pitch. He proudly took them into the hushed scriptorium where monks and scribes bent over their sloping desks, patiently translating and copying from books which were brought to them by a couple of assistants, who tiptoed to and from the shelves where the large heavy tomes were kept chained when not in use. Peter looked over one scribe's shoulder and was amazed at the exactitude of the copy he was making of a page in a Latin herbarium. He watched entranced as the replica of a sword-lily emerged from what seemed like just a few deft strokes of the brush. Someone else was copying a translation of an Arabic treatise on astronomy, in which Porcarius pointed out to him the picture of an astrolabe. The strange Arabic script seemed to Peter frivolous and random, itself a scatter of stars across the parchment.

The boys felt sorry to take leave of their congenial uncle the next day, aware now of just how much road still lay ahead of them, for the journey to the Paraclete was likely to take about another ten days, weather and road conditions permitting. They rode cautiously for fear of tiring the horses, stopping at a tavern each evening at dusk, and rising at first light to make the most of the short November days.

The road took them to the north of the Ardusson valley, via Provins, famous for its great trading fairs which the Count of Champagne encouraged in order to bring wealth to his lands. Although the two main fairs at Provins were held in May and September, it was a busy and thriving town at all times of the year. Peter, Charles and Fulk were amazed at the confusion, the colours, the crowds, which teemed and thronged in the long main market-place and in the tiny streets. They left the horses at an inn, and walked around in a daze, Peter tightly clutching the bag containing his rebec and the little offerings for Heloise, aware that it might at any moment be snatched from him. He had never seen so many types of craftsmen in so small an area; every doorway seemed to be occupied by someone who was either making or selling something, whether it was blacksmith or barber, wheelwright or weaver, tailor or tanner. And no one was too busy or too absorbed to prevent them calling out, almost continuously it seemed, in support of their wares. Mules and handcarts laden with barrels of ale or bales of cloth were pushed and pulled in all directions, but they never seemed to collide despite the narrowness of the lanes. People leant out of upstairs windows shouting to one another, and in one place, where the houses leant over at such an angle that the street below was almost a tunnel, two women, one from each side, were shaking hands.

Near the priory of St Ayoul, which Porcarius had advised them to visit because Abelard had once taken refuge there, a small crowd of people stood around watching an acrobat, who was attempting to walk a tight-rope strung across the street between a house-window and one of the priory's gargoyles. At one point, the rope crossed a drain, whose foetid smell must have added to the man's incentive not to fall. Beside him a dwarf beat out a rhythm on a tabor; Peter glanced at him, and then looked again more keenly. Surely this was the same dwarf who'd been to Le Pallet with a couple of musicians earlier in the year? He remembered the evening well; they had unwittingly sung one of Abelard's old love-songs, sending Peter out in furious retreat to the refuge of his apple tree.

171

Louis had sniggered, Charles had come out to pacify him and Aunt Denise had dismissed the performers. Dear Aunt Denise – no doubt she'd be thinking about them at this very moment, anxiously wondering where they were. And Nicolette – what would she be doing? She had Louis more or less to herself now. Did he know how she felt about him? Would he take advantage of her? Would she ever think of Peter in his absence?

Charles didn't agree that it was the same dwarf, however, and Peter began to lose interest in the display. He preferred watching the people going about their business. What struck him was that everyone seemed to be in a hurry, and walked or ran at least twice as fast as at Le Pallet. He'd been to Nantes quite often of course, but even the port there lacked the variety and vitality of this meeting place between merchants from the weaving towns of Flanders and those of the trading towns all over France, Germany and Italy. Always attracted by music, Peter found himself drawn to the sound of pan pipes; he wandered off on his own down the market-place until he found the piper. Two dogs teetered and staggered on their hind legs while the children in the front of the group of onlookers clapped a sort of rhythm to the pipe-music. It was a pathetic tawdry show, and someone expressed their disappointment by throwing a rotten apple at one of the dogs. It landed on its prominent ribs and with a howl the creature dropped both pretence and forelegs, to slink behind its scowling and no longer piping master. Behind him in a darkened doorway, Peter caught sight of a tall narrow wooden cage into which a bear had been crammed, half-sitting, half-standing, for it could do neither in comfort. Peter guessed the bear's turn was next, but he had no wish to stay and see the creature's total humiliation. Strange, the things that some people enjoyed, he thought, as he walked away more in puzzlement than in pity.

He rejoined the other two, and together they made their way towards the upper town and the main ramparts. As they walked up the steep winding street an unfamiliar noise met them from above.

"Lepers," said Fulk importantly, for he recognized the sound from his recent pilgrimage. And sure enough, as they rounded the bend, they came face to face with a small band of brown-hooded lepers, their leather-thonged clapper-boards in shrill, menacing clamour. Peter shrank instinctively from the piteous sight and insistent din, edging into the side of the street to leave as much of the passageway between them and him as possible. But he couldn't help taking another half-repelled, half-fascinated look at them as they passed; the front two seemed to be oldish men, though it was hard to judge their age behind the white crumbly shrivel of their faces. But it was the one bringing up the rear who made the big impression on him. His nose had almost disappeared, but one could still tell that he was a young man of only about nineteen or twenty. He carried himself with pride, his clapper-board the only one to hang silent. His fine dark blue eyes seemed to bore through Peter as the lepers passed by, leaving him feeling somehow accused. By what strange act of grace had God chosen that other young man to walk in the rough brown hemp of a leper's shroud, while he – a forgotten son, after all – rode in the fine cloth of garments made for him with affection and with care?

It was two days later when Peter left Nogent-sur-Seine on the last stage of his journey to the Paraclete. Charles, who had been warned by Denise of the need for great tact in this matter, suggested, despite his curiosity to see Heloise himself, that he and Fulk should stay in Nogent to rest the horses for a day or two and that Peter should rejoin them when he was ready. The abbey was remote and they were assured in Nogent that the chance of being attacked during those last few miles was very small. The valley of the Ardusson was dark and marshy and thickly wooded; as Peter rode along he was conscious of the sound of fast-flowing water, yet the river was completely concealed behind trees and scrub. The November sun, low and spiteful on the horizon, dazzled his eyes without warming him or brightening the landscape. Peter looked in vain for similarities to that other river valley he knew so well.

As he eventually turned left off the road onto the track which was signed for the abbey of the Paraclete, he thought his stomach must feel something like the new eel-trap in the mill-race at home. Peggy, subdued by the long days of travelling, kept her head nearly steady and plodded obediently. The sound of rushing water grew louder, but still there was no visible sign of the river, so well guarded by its wooded banks. The track suddenly turned sharply to the right, led over a narrow stream, which presumably fed into the Ardusson, and then stopped altogether before a gate in a long low wall. Behind the gate was a wooden hut, a cross nailed beside its door.

After a little pause, Peter pulled at the iron bell and then jumped for it seemed to send a strident jangle clanging through his very bloodstream. For a few moments nothing happened and he was just plucking up courage to pull again when a small pink-faced nun in late middle-age appeared. She looked at him in a curious but not unfriendly way, and asked him politely what his business was.

"I've come to speak to the abbess of the Paraclete," he heard his voice state unwaveringly.

"I'm afraid, sir, that the Reverend Mother is at her

studies now and cannot be disturbed. And the sacristan and other officers are all in chapel, and I had no instruction to allow anyone in today except the priest who shall say Mass for us." But she seemed so ready to talk that Peter was not discouraged.

"I . . . Please tell her it's very urgent." Peter was amazed at himself. But suddenly he did feel the urgency of the moment; he'd waited almost sixteen years for this, and another sixteen minutes would be too long. The portress, who was a little too persuadable for her job, heard the command in his voice and said:

"Excuse me, sir, who shall I say . . ?"

"Please tell her that it's a messenger from Le Pallet."

"If you would be kind enough to wait, sir."

Peter walked up and down impatiently outside the gate as Peggy cropped the wet grass. He didn't have long to wait before the portress bustled back, flushed with the unusual exertion, or enjoyment of the break in routine, or both.

"If you please, sir, you may wait inside. Mother will be with you forthwith."

He stood as if for support against the triangular lip of a small well and surveyed the scene. Over to his right was a farmyard, surrounded by barns and store-houses, and he could just see the corner of a pond and a couple of sleepy ducks. Ahead of him was a small stone abbey with a cloistered walkway, built on three sides of a square. Still he was bothered by the sound of water which he couldn't see. It was a damp, cheerless, low-lying place; Peter thought of how Abelard and his one or two loyal followers had built a makeshift settle-ment from nothing; how it was the energy and devo-tion of his students which had gradually given the place the permanence of stone. And later Abelard had himself given the property over to Heloise and her sister nuns, to be in turn their refuge when they were made

175

homeless by their former convent in Argenteuil. Yet even knowing all that, it was hard to think of it as a place of sanctuary, of comfort: it meant nothing to him, Peter, who compared it unfavourably with the open blowy view from Boundary Ridge and the flowering orchards and water meadows of the Sanguèze valley. He forgot that back in Brittany the fruit-trees would also be bare by now, and the meadows soggy from the first floods of winter.

As he waited, Peter kept a wary eye on a door in the angle of the abbey walls through which he'd seen the portress disappear earlier. Behind him he was aware of Peggy moving from one patch of grass to another and giving intermittent little snorts; and he couldn't fail to hear the squabble of crows, which sent the few remaining leaves showering in all directions from a group of elms by the farmyard wall. But so intent was he on watching the first door that he neither saw nor heard another door open from the wing of the abbey which was nearest to the hidden river.

And so Heloise came unnoticed towards him. He didn't see the worried frown on her face as she wondered what tidings awaited her from Le Pallet; nor did he see her swift step falter or her eyes close in the moment of long-awaited shock, when she first saw her young visitor at the well.

A few yards away she called softly: "Peter Astralabe?" with only the slightest hint of query in her voice. And when he turned, startled, and she saw his face with its wide grey eyes, there was no longer any doubt.

He dropped to his knee, relieved to hide his confusion in the little ritual of courtesy.

She spoke gently, but without a tremor.

"Come, rise, let me look at you."

So he looked at her, shyly, while for one long moment she searched his face almost hungrily. If she's

176

looking for a likeness to Abelard, she would have been better pleased with Louis, thought Peter. And the eels still raced in the trap of his stomach.

"And the news from home, Le Pallet?"

"Everyone is well. There's no urgent message – I just didn't know what to say . . ."

"Of course."

"But – are you travelling alone? Surely not?"

"No. Charles and someone from the village have come with me. We're going to take Charles to study at Chartres. But they've stayed behind in Nogent . . . to rest the horses."

Heloise nodded, appreciating the tact. "So little Charles is to study at Chartres!" She smiled and shook her head, and then fell silent, aware that an even greater transformation than that from toddler to student stood in the flesh before her.

The silence persisted, all the imagined rehearsals of little help to either of them now that the meeting was finally taking place.

Then, lifting her hands in a delayed gesture of welcome, she said, a smile lighting up her eyes: "I'm forgetting my manners. You must be hungry? And thirsty?"

"No, thank you." Again this problem of not knowing the right form of address. He was undoubtedly the only person at this place who could not call her 'Mother'.

"But I thought all young men were hungry and thirsty all the time!"

"Well, I am most of the time – but not just now." He smiled back – and found that it was surprisingly easy.

"Yes, I understand." A little laugh; a small pause. Then, "It's not normal practice, of course, but would you like to see around the grounds? We could start now, while the sisters are still in chapel for they

177

shouldn't see you."

Peter agreed gratefully; it would make it all much easier if they were walking around and looking at things.

"Come, we'll start with the farm. It'll remind you of home. Perhaps you should tether your pony first." She watched him as he did so. "Isn't it rather small for such a long journey?"

"Yes, but we've had a long partnership. She's my favourite. And no one else can really manage her," he added with a tinge of pride, remembering only afterwards, with a little jolt of guilt, his recent spectacular fall.

"So tell me about the journey. How long has it taken you?" she asked as they walked towards the farmyard. Peter found himself telling her about the visit to Porcarius and the scriptorium in Angers, about the Arabic treatise with its picture of the astrolabe, about the half-familiar dwarf and the colourful crowds in Provins. Part of him seemed for a moment to escape from his body, as it had back in Lambert's hut on that terrible afternoon, and looking down at himself he marvelled at the ease with which he talked to the unfamiliar lady in the nun's habit, who walked in step beside him. He felt the frequency of her glances, but she didn't stare through him making him feel shrivelled and empty.

They passed the bakehouse and Peter sniffed the aroma of new-baked bread.

"Ah, we are not permitted the pleasure of new bread fresh from the oven, but you as a visitor shall have some," she promised, with another of the smiles which lit up her face.

She asked after all the members of the family – all, that is, except one – and even seemed to want to know about Ralph and Agatha and Agnes whom she'd never

178

seen. He thought suddenly of the little gifts in his saddle-bag and his precious rebec.

"Will the saddlebag be safe?" he asked suddenly, interrupting himself.

"Yes, no one will touch them here. There're only the sisters and the few lay brothers who do the heavier farmwork for us. We seldom receive visitors or pilgrims. Life is very sober and quiet at the Paraclete." Very quickly she went on, "Those barns there are the original ones – you see they're built with mud and rushes. Ah, the sisters are coming out of Mass. It's better that we wait here, out of sight."

As they stood and waited they looked at each other. Heloise was about a head shorter than Peter, her build – hidden in the shapeless folds of religious dress – seemed slight. And Maud had been right: her eyes, fringed in their long dark lashes, *were* very beautiful and very sad. Peter realized that, almost in spite of himself, he *liked* her. She was direct, open, friendly. Her pleasure at seeing him was very evident, yet she hadn't intruded on him by calling him 'son' or demanding an embrace; nor had she retreated from him, leaving him alone and undefended.

When the sisters had returned to the main abbey buildings in their customary silence, she turned to him again.

"I should really ask you whether you prefer to be addressed as 'Astralabe' or 'Peter'?"

He looked down and said almost apologetically, "Well, I *am* used to Peter." If she were disappointed she didn't allow it to show.

After only the slightest pause, she continued, "Then Peter it is. Tell me, do you like music?"

"I love music."

"I thought that was a strong possibility." It was the first reference, if a very oblique one, to Abelard.

"Come. I've something to show you, then. Have you ever seen an organistrum? We've just acquired one – Sister Paula, our chantress, persuaded me that it would improve our poor vocal offerings to the Lord beyond recognition – and I think she was right."

The chapel was surrounded by trees on a piece of raised ground some fifty yards behind the abbey. Heloise showed him the instrument and, while he examined it and worked out for himself how between them the two players would operate the little wheel which rubbed the string and the keys which stopped it, she knelt at the simple altar. Peter could only guess at the content of her prayer, but after a few minutes he went and knelt in silence beside her.

He followed her down the short steep path from the chapel door.

"Peter," she said as they reached the bottom and faced each other again, "I'm so glad you've come. I wondered when it would be." There was a new tenderness in her voice, but instead of soothing him it seemed suddenly to unlock the store of feelings that had lain meek and dormant beneath the small talk of Le Pallet and Provins in the world outside.

All at once he blurted out, "Why did you never send me word? Why am I not mentioned in your letters? And only barely in Abelard's account of his troubles?"

Again crows clattered in the tree-tops above them; from somewhere in the farmyard, obscured now by the wooded hillock, a cow lowed. Then, apart from the unseen river, everything was quiet.

"Peter, if I didn't send you word of greeting or advice, it wasn't due to indifference – it didn't occur to me that . . ." Suddenly a look of horror spread across her fine regular features, so like Peter's own. For the words she used had a horrible intimate familiarity. She saw before her momentarily closed eyes a vision of

Abelard's writing, making the same paltry excuses in response to her own reproaches.

*If . . . I have not yet written you any word of comfort or advice, it must not be attributed to indifference on my part but to your own good sense, in which I have always had such confidence that I did not think anything was needed.*

"So . . . this too, this too," she whispered, as if only now understanding the full scale of the sacrifice she had made. Helplessly, Peter watched the slow passage of grief across her face.

"So have *you* felt forgotten and deserted? Tell me, you must tell me." Her tone was urgent.

He nodded dumbly. He couldn't retreat now; the forgotten son of the eunuch and his holy whore was at last having his revenge – and hating every second of it.

"Peter – my *son*." For the first time she named the relationship between them, perhaps because only now did she recognize the loss contained in the word. They were still standing facing one another, tense and straight. Her headdress blew a little in the breeze. "When I was a young woman I made up my mind to do as Abe–lard wished, to give my life to God. Believe me, it was no sense of vocation which brought me to accept the strict relentless life of the cloister, but *his* bidding, and that alone. I have done nothing as yet for God, but only for the love of . . . Abe–lard, your earthly father." Peter noticed how she pronounced his name – with the briefest hiatus between the 'e' and the 'lard' as if to keep the name a little longer on her lips. "I sacrificed all my joy, not only in him, but also in motherhood." She looked down, unable to meet his eyes any longer.

'Heloise had agreed to take the veil, in obedience to my wishes.' For all his earlier anger, it was only now that Peter really felt the cruel weight of those few brief words.

"In the last few years I began to wonder more and more about you and how you would receive and interpret our story. But I never suspected that in giving up motherhood, I might have sacrificed my child as well. So I never even wrote to you." She shook her head as if in disbelief.

Peter felt pity hurt him in the way he imagined a weapon wound might hurt. He would never before have believed it possible to feel such a thing on behalf of another person.

He began to glimpse how for fifteen years she had borne in dignity, silence and devotion to duty a passion and a loneliness which were beyond most other people's experience. Perhaps, he reflected, his own capacity for passionate love was her unique legacy.

And she, now face to face with the living proof, recognized that in loving one person too much she had failed to love another enough; she had condemned her son, standing at last tense and white-faced before her, to grow up in the shadow of her own loss. That had not been right. He had had a claim on her which she had neither recognized nor fulfilled.

"I didn't come to reproach you," said Peter gently, yet he knew he lied. He remembered the hate that had thrilled in his blood as he raced across Boundary Ridge before his fall; he remembered too the many tears of hot bewildered rage which he'd shed in the little apple tree. No, there'd been more to this pilgrimage than a desire to know and understand. In truth, it had been more of a crusade; he had, after all, ridden across France with righteous indignation in his head and an unnamed longing in his heart.

But the gentle lie lowered the tension between them and she said, "Come, there's a seat along here by the side of the field." And added, as if apologizing for the luxury, "It's for the sisters to rest from their labour at

182

harvest-time."

As she sat down she asked, "Was it your own idea to come here now?" Looking down into her face he thought how lovely she was for a woman of her age, with her high brow and clear, smooth skin – and those sad beautiful eyes, only slightly marked by lines. He said, "My father Peter Abelard came to visit and when he left he expressed the desire that I should come. He wanted me to bring some laments he has written. But I'd wanted to come anyway – for a long time, I think. His wish served only as my spur."

"That was nicely put." Again she searched his face with a sort of hunger. "You saw Abe–lard? At Le Pallet?"

"Yes. He has left St Gildas now and was on his way back to Paris to resume his teaching there. He left copies of your letters and the *Historia Calamitatum*. And the laments – which I've brought for you."

"At his wish?"

"At his wish. It was one of the last things he said to me as he rode away. 'Take the *Planctus* with you – it's right you should do that.' "

"Did he spend long with you?"

"Perhaps a week. Not more."

"And how was his health? Has he recovered from that fall from his horse? Did you talk of many things? Did he teach you at all?"

Peter now sat down himself.

"Please slow down. I'm not sure what to answer first!" They both laughed then in a moment of pure mutual understanding.

"It's unfair of me to ask so much, but I receive so little news. It'll soon be five years since he left, after settling us into this place which he gave us in his great charity. And even then," she added very quietly, "nothing personal passed between us. That seemed to be his will."

"I'll tell you everything, with all my heart. But I'm

183

afraid there's not *so* much to tell."

"Soon it will be time for chapel again. Will you stay here tonight? The visitors' quarters are quite comfortable but I'm afraid you're not permitted to eat with us."

"I'd be honoured."

"Then we'll talk again later. Just tell me one little thing first."

"If I can, I will."

"Is his hair now all white? And . . . no, I cannot ask you that."

"Yes, it is – more or less – completely greyish-white." He spoke carefully, thinking back, anxious not to mislead her. "But continue, pray."

"Does . . . well, does it still curl a little around his ears?" Tears now fell freely down her cheeks, as at the same time she laughed at her own folly. "How *could* I ask you such a thing? *I* who am in charge of the moral and spiritual welfare of more than forty souls. I despise myself as he would despise me for such a lewd thought – I will do a fitting penance."

Peter leant forward spontaneously and took her in his arms. Tears pricked at the back of his own eyes, even though – or perhaps because – he was now a man. For he had understood that those curls of Abelard's hair, which he too had noticed while sitting as a pupil beside him, were to Heloise what a certain arrow-head birthmark was to him. "*I* don't despise you for it. I rather love you for it. And – yes, it does!" Heloise, with her extraordinary honesty, her intuition, her readiness to listen and understand, her pleasure in seeing him, her guilt and her sorrow had worked on what remained of his resentment and his self-pity more effectively than sun on any morning fog. Truly, God had saved him from that fall for a purpose.

"Surely, God has granted me a consolation I didn't

deserve." She was holding his hand and studying it, still through a blur. "I left it to someone else to wipe away all your childish tears, yet you've come to help me dry my old untimely ones!"

Peter left the Paraclete the next day, but not before they had 'shared', in Heloise's word, a first unpractised performance by the choir and organistrum of one of the laments. She chose the one in which David mourns the death of his beloved friend Jonathan. For propriety's sake Peter had to stand concealed behind a screen, and so it was separately, from different positions within the church, that mother and son heard King David's song of suffering rise up on the wings of Abelard's poetry into the timber roof, where Peter watched the slow, sad dance of shadows.

> '. . . And to live after thee
> Is but to die
> For with but half a soul what can life do?'

"His gift for poetry is greater than ever," Heloise observed afterwards, her voice soft with wonder. They were walking by then towards the gate, the sisters inside the abbey now resting before nones.

In a more matter-of-fact tone she continued after a pause, "Tell Maud that of course I couldn't forget her. She's right, as she usually is, about my need for strength – but tell her, too, that in the last day I have been happier than at any time in fifteen years. It's not today I shall need her cordial."

The portress watched them, intrigued. She enjoyed her privileged position at the gate lodge, a meeting place of two worlds, and the opportunity it gave for observation.

"And to Denise. What message can I send to my

dearest sister Denise other than . . . I shall always keep the little blanket in memory of the baby who was ours, Abe–lard's and mine. But now I return to her with love and gratitude the fine young man who in the flesh is my son, her nephew; in truth he is her son, my friend."

The portress saw the young man kneel and kiss Mother Superior's hand in respectful though rather prolonged farewell. She had never seen anyone do that before, and wondered if it were quite proper; but Mother, whose hand rested lightly on the young man's head, knew best about such things. Then she opened the gate to let him pass, and watched him ride over the makeshift wooden bridge, which crossed the tiny tributary to the Ardusson and marked the boundary of the Paraclete's land.

Peter was turning left towards the road, when he realized with a little shock of dismay that he hadn't shown Heloise the rebec still hanging in his saddlebag. She would have liked that. He stopped and went back, wondering if there were still time. But through the gate he saw she was already walking away towards the abbey and the hundred duties which awaited her there. Beyond her, through a small break in the dense barren scrub which hid its course throughout much of the long valley, he caught his first and only glimpse of the river. Somehow, despite the dull November light, it seemed to shine.

# SHADOW OF THE WALL

## Christa Laird

*"There's only one way which is reasonably safe, Misha, and it's not very pleasant." Misha sat back on the pile of newspapers... Sheer physical panic seized him, beginning in his feet and rising up like an electric current through his limbs.*

*"Not ... the sewers?" he croaked.*

It's spring 1942, and life in the Warsaw ghetto is hard and often brutal, with the Jews subject to beatings and execution at the hands of the hated SS. Young Misha lives at the Orphans' Home run by the heroic Dr Korczak. But the time is fast approaching when Misha must prove himself a hero too...

"A story full of excitement and compassion."
*Geoffrey Trease*
*The Times Educational Supplement*

"A book to make you cry."
*Jessica Yates, The Daily Telegraph*

# KNIGHTS OF THE SACRED BLADE
## Julian Atterton

In the warring Britain of 1135, the kingdom of Northumbria faces destruction. Young Simon de Falaise and Aimeric the scholar set out on a perilous quest to find "The Sacred Blade" – an ancient sword with the power, according to legend, to save their homeland. Others, however, are also searching...

"Julian Atterton is one of the brightest stars in the galaxy of young historical writers."
*Christina Hardyment, The Independent*

"Julian Atterton writes with power and clarity, his clean-cut prose glinting with flashes of poetry."
*Geoffrey Trease*
*The Times Educational Supplement*

"Political intrigue, romance and deeds of courage are woven together in this fast moving tale."
*Valerie Bierman, The Scotsman*

# THE TRIPLE SPIRAL

## Stephanie Green

*The wind rose to a howl and in it was the baying of the infernal hounds. The reeds hissed like snakes. Moddy Dhu crouched, snarling, his teeth bared, his eyes evil, red slits.*

When Sonia and her family move into an isolated windmill in Norfolk, they find the area rife with legend and superstition. Preoccupied with their own domestic tensions, the Carrs have little time for stories about a Moon Goddess, a demon dog or a terrible flood. Gradually, though, these "myths" start to take on a very real and terrifying signi-ficance…

"This first novel, multi-layered, complex, elegantly structured as it is, manages to grip almost from the first page… A beautifully constructed ghost story."
*Books for Your Children*

"The scenes of family life are original and provocative." *The Times Educational Supplement*

# BROTHER NIGHT

## Victor Kelleher

*He looked up and saw two pale half-moons. Two!*
*Eyes staring at him. A face hanging there in the*
*gloom. So awful a face that he screamed and*
*screamed again...*

Ramon has been brought up as the son of a village
gate-keeper. One night, though, he is told his true
parentage: his mother is the Moon Witch and his
father the all-powerful Sun Lord. More disturbing
still, he learns that he was one of twins, his monstrous
brother apparently destroyed at birth. But nothing,
as Ramon soon discovers, is this black and white –
what seems dark may be light, what seems good may
be evil. One thing, however, *is* certain: finding out the
truth is going to be a very perilous and challenging
quest indeed...

"A robust and thought-provoking fantasy... Power-
fully imagined... Fast paced and full of action."
*Neil Philip, The Times Educational Supplement*

# MORE WALKER PAPERBACKS
## For You to Enjoy